THE WAYWARD RING

WITCHES OF MARIGOLD
BOOK TWO

SONIA ORIN LYRIS

KNOTTED ROAD PRESS

CHAPTER
ONE

"Mom?" Nicholas asked the air.

Don't be a baby, he told himself.

Nicholas Gaffon looked over his backyard fence onto an overgrown acre of alder, maple, and fir. The ground beyond was thick with brown and yellow leaves.

A cool day for autumn, though not so cold that thirteen-year-old Nicholas needed a jacket.

He looked for the source of the strange sound, his breath coming short and shallow, arm raised, clutching a rock, ready to throw.

Something like a call. Or a moan. What was it?

The fence at which he stood tilted outward. Once, it had been painted gray or maybe brown. Now it was little more than rotting wood and rusted nails.

The breeze shifted. For a moment, Nicholas caught a whiff of a burn pile from the rural farms outside town, woodsmoke and something else, not quite as nice. Tires, maybe.

Then the sound was back. It hissed across the ground as if dragging an invisible tail, raising leaves in a line.

It stopped ten feet from where Nicholas stood. He gripped the rock tightly.

Whatever it was turned to look at him, with a face that wasn't really a face. It spoke to him, maybe shouted, but without words. There was a feeling, too. Something like fury.

Terrified, Nicholas closed his eyes.

This isn't happening.

His eyes sprang open again.

It was gone. No moving leaves. No hissing. No eyes that weren't really eyes.

Nicholas curled in on himself, crumpling down to his hands and knees in the muddy grass, the rock dropped and forgotten. He heaved once, dry.

Am I crazy?

He gazed down at the overgrown grass, then got to his feet, wiping muddy hands across jeans, brushing sandy grit from his fingertips on his dark green flannel shirt.

His eyes flickered over the fence. Nothing.

What was that?

For sure not his mother. He put a hand on the outside of his pants pocket, feeling the metal of his ring through the fabric. Her ring.

Into his mind flashed his mother's face and smile, nothing like the angry glare of that weird thing out there.

Then the image that always wanted to take over the screen of his mind, that moment when the paramedics carried her out of the house, her body covered with a gray blanket.

He remembered thinking: *I can't see her face. So it can't be her.*

Then, absurdly, he remembered how she used to fry him eggs in butter. He hadn't eaten eggs since then. He would give up eggs for the rest of his life to have her back.

The worst part was how he kept expecting her to walk into the house after work. Then he would know who he was again, what he was supposed to do with his life.

"Nick?" his father called from the back door.

Nicholas didn't move.

"Nick."

He exhaled, turned around. His father stood at the single-step stoop of the back door, arms crossed over an open navy-blue windbreaker, showing a stained white t-shirt beneath.

Mom would never have let him wear that.

"What are you doing out here?" his father asked in a flat tone.

Used to be, he could tell his father anything.

"Nothing."

For a moment, neither spoke.

"Dinner in forty."

Nicholas nodded, slowly walking through the muddy grass to the house. He could feel his father's stare. When he was halfway there, his father turned and went inside, letting the screen door slam shut behind him, as if he'd forgotten Nicholas entirely.

Nicholas paused at the stoop and gave a look over his shoulder at the fence.

Branches of maple, alder, and Douglas fir. Nothing more.

CHAPTER

TWO

"It sure is quiet," Rufus said in a hushed voice.

"That's the idea," Keyton said, looking up at the top of the utility pole.

Rufus squinted up and down Main Street. Marigold was a small enough town that it wasn't particularly unusual for the street to be empty, as it was now.

But the three teenagers knew they had to be certain, so they had come out at five am.

Rufus yawned. *Only for friends,* he thought, staring at Angie.

Angie shook her head, which meant the beaded tips of her braids made a soft tapping sound together. They were the magenta ones, Rufus was pretty sure, though it was hard to tell in this dim light. Sometimes he got close enough to her to get a scent. She smelled warm, like cardamom with a hint of allspice. Was it weird that he liked how she smelled?

"That one's better," Angie said, pointing down the street.

"Why?" Rufus asked quietly.

There was something about the silent morning that made Rufus speak softly, even if it was just them.

"Hardware store doesn't block the prevailing winds," Angie said.

"Ang is right. Line of sight." Keyton said.

"Oh, a rhyme!" Rufus said, brightening, and smiling at Angie.

Keyton laughed. "Come on."

The trio headed south, passing the darkened windows of the hardware store, then the Four Forks diner with its three stripes of red, orange, and yellow blanched of color in the dark.

"We should reward ourselves later," said Keyton, eyeing the Snowball's Chance Creamery right next to Four Forks.

Rufus sneered. "Kid stuff. You want really good ice cream, you have to go to Poly's in Cottonwood Creek."

"Yeah? You driving yet?" Keyton asked. "And I remember you going on about the squid-ink ice cream. Gross."

"It wasn't that bad," Rufus replied. "Or that good."

They stopped at the next pole.

"We sure this is a sensible plan?" Angie asked.

"Yep," Keyton replied, setting down a bundle of climbing equipment at the base. "I watched a bunch of videos."

"How many is a bunch?" Angie asked.

"At least three," Keyton replied.

"Maybe I should do it," said Rufus, taking from his pack the weather station rig they'd pooled their money to buy at a local swap meet.

"I'm smarter," said Keyton.

"I'm bigger," Rufus said, feeling slightly annoyed.

Keyton turned to face Rufus. "How many videos did you watch?"

Rufus pushed out his lower jaw. "None. But I know how to climb."

"This? With this equipment?" asked Keyton, pointing at the harness and leg climbers that ze had brought.

While Rufus considered his answer, Keyton stepped into the butt-harness, snugging it up, and snapping the belt around zir waist and then around the pole. "Anyway, we already agreed. Next time you watch the vids and you can."

"If anything bad happens to you," Angie said, "Sanne is going to kill us for being idiots."

"Then let's make sure nothing bad happens," Keyton said.

Keyton's expression went serious. "You know what? Say a spell for me, okay?"

Rufus felt it, how things shifted between them and so suddenly. Their gazes flickered to each other.

"You bet," said Angie, taking Rufus's hand.

Which felt really good.

The three of them linked hands in a circle. Angie spoke softly, a spell of uniting and collaboration.

Rufus was somewhat certain she was making it up, but she sounded so good that he wouldn't have been surprised if she had found it in one of Sanne's books and memorized it. Angie was good at so many things.

Angie inhaled, then added under her breath that the three of them were aiming to do good for the town by helping track the weather, so maybe the spirits, if any were around, could lend them some luck?

Rufus and Angie stepped back to give Keyton room. Keyton fastened the spiked cuffs to zir ankles and buckled the brace to just below zir knees.

Keyton took a breath, leaned back to take the slack out of the belt, sunk a spiked foot into the pole, and began to climb.

Sanne's mobile rang.

No, it didn't. It emitted the caw of a spotted towhee, which then became the bird's lovely staccato trill. Sanne had recorded the audio one morning at dawn in the forest, and it was perfect.

Sanne cocked her head, letting the feel and flow of the caller enter into her awareness.

Few people actually called her. Her sister Marla, and sometimes Della.

Della who was off in Canada with her newlywed husband Terry, at a real estate conference, followed by a lengthy honeymoon.

Sanne missed Della. It surprised her to miss the other woman, given how unlikely the friendship had been to begin with. They had started as adversaries, and were forced to work together to keep immensely powerful and dangerous demon eggs from hatching and destroying the town of Marigold.

Once they knew each other that well, they started to like each other.

Then, months ago, under the not-quite-full moon of early summer, the demon egg enchantment was finalized. Della and Sanne and the three teenagers stood in a circle on the recently cured concrete, atop the two demon eggs, weaving a spell to make sure they would never hatch, and if they did, they would never emerge.

The eggs were solidly ensorcelled now, contained in the magical equivalent of deep freeze, sealed into holes like vaults beneath physical stone and magical concrete.

A fine night's work that had been.

A work of art, really. A beautiful spell that drew from the area's deep ancient magma and the root system of trees. Rufus had brought the carpet of fungus that was everywhere, from mushroom to lichen. Angie drew spores and microscopic flora that lived on the breeze. And Keyton invoked the moisture in the air, the aquifer, and the cement itself. Keyton had announced that for the duration of the spell, ze was moving into zir masculine energy so as to balance the female-leaning group, and to stand alongside Rufus.

Sanne was lucky beyond reason for the kids. For the forest.

Even for Della. But the call didn't have Della's scent. Nor Marla's.

She swiped up.

"Hello," she said.

"Susanne Pascral?" asked a male voice.

Someone who didn't know her well enough to know her friend-name.

"Yes?" she asked.

A moment's silence.

"I don't know how to say this, so I'll just spit it out. I'm your brother. My name is Allen."

Sanne blinked, and blinked again.

"I have a brother?"

"We getting weather reports from the rig yet?" Rufus asked. He laced his fingers through the chain link surrounding the Marigold Middle School play yard.

Sapling trees lined the street just outside the fence, but the play yard was otherwise flat concrete, with faded paint that would have been perfect for some elementary school games like four-square, mini-softball, hopscotch.

Late morning recess. Rufus caught a brief whiff of burnt food from a cafeteria vent. The lasagna, from the scent of it.

"Should be," Keyton muttered unhappily. "But something's wrong with the transmitter."

Angie was staring. Rufus followed her gaze across the yard. Four girls on two benches bent toward each other, whispering and pointing at them.

Rufus looked back. The girls giggled. It wasn't the nice kind of laughter.

"We're the weird ones now," Angie said softly.

"And I used to be so popular," Rufus said dryly.

Keyton snorted in amusement. Rufus grinned wide. So many of his jokes fell flat that to get one airborne felt good.

Of course, making Angie laugh would be even better, though it wasn't something she did easily.

Rufus noted that the magenta beads on her dreadlocks alternated with yellow, which was really nice.

"I wonder why it's mostly girls," Angie said. "Boys gossip, too, don't they?" This was directed at Rufus.

Keyton raised zir eyebrows and gave Rufus a sour look.

"Sure we do," Rufus said. "My dad gossips all the time about other people in Marigold and what's wrong with them."

"People like me and my parents?" asked Angie, in that call-it-out-but-gently tone she was so good at.

Angie's dark skin attracted attention in the very white town of Marigold, along with comments that were just soft enough that you couldn't quite make them out.

And yet, somehow, Angie didn't get angry. Sometimes Rufus wished she would.

Rufus nodded a little, reluctantly. "Used to. Not any more." Not since Rufus started pushing back.

"How'd you talk your dad into enrolling you here?" Keyton asked him.

"I pointed out to him," Rufus answered, "that I should get some experience talking with other kids, kids I didn't already know, so I could be better at networking, which would matter once I got my degree in business."

"Really?" Angie asked, looking impressed.

Inwardly Rufus preened. This day was getting better and better.

"Yeah, just like that," Rufus said.

"Sanne help you prep for it?" Keyton asked with a smirk.

While Rufus was chewing on what would be a clever reply to that all-too-on-the-nose guess, the end-of-recess bell rang.

The three kids walked toward the school door, where they would go their separate ways for classes before meeting again after school, and going together over to Sanne's house for an hour or two of tutoring. Maybe some knitting, even.

Rufus's next class was math. He wasn't sure he liked it, but he knew that—kind of like oatmeal—it would someday be good for him.

Especially if you want to go into game design, Sanne had told him the other night.

He liked how Sanne could be so practical and direct, willing to tell him what aspects of school he'd need to know and which he could kind of sleep through.

They were ambling back in a crowd of teenagers toward the building, Keyton chatting about some movie ze wanted to watch. Some kids streamed around them to get in front, some trailed behind.

The three were just passing through the open, black metal double doors, when a boy even taller than Rufus, his back to them, stepped backward from just inside the school at the moment that Keyton, looking at Rufus and Angie, stepped forward.

They bounced off each other.

Keyton said, "Watch where you're going, Sasquatch."

The boy turned around. He scowled.

Rufus was big for his age. This kid was bigger. He had brown hair, a blue shirt under a yellow blazer. He held his hands chest-high and balled them into fists.

Rufus had only been at Marigold Middle School for a couple months, but he had noticed Nicholas Gaffon right away, the way you did when you were larger than average and knew that made you a target. Especially with other big kids.

Rufus had been spared most of that weirdness, having been home-schooled. Sure, he'd witnessed boys getting in each other's faces at the park, and once in a while in the back yard at the church. Rufus's father had grown up boxing, had tried to get Rufus to train, and finally gave up. Rufus wasn't into it.

So while Rufus had never been in a fight that went beyond words, he knew what the start looked like. The challenging posture. The threatening tone.

Nicholas lowered his head to glare down at the much shorter Keyton. "What did you say?"

"Maybe you could not block the damned door, tool," Keyton muttered softly, but not so softly that Rufus didn't hear.

And Nicholas, too, judging by his tightening expression.

"Oh, look," said Nicholas loudly enough to be heard by the gathering crowd. "It's the kid who can't tell she's a girl." He gave a small, mock-bow to Keyton and swept a hand toward the school hallway beyond. "After you, little miss weirdo."

When Rufus thought about it later—and he would have lots of time to think about it later, sitting in the principal's office— that had been the inflection point, the moment at which everything could have gone just fine instead.

Really, all Keyton would have needed to do was shrug it off and walk past Nicholas. Then the four of them could have gone to their classes, finished the school day, and joined Sanne for lessons. Maybe even some knitting.

But that's not what Keyton did.

FOUR

"Oh, for fuck's sake," said Marla on the phone, with precise punctuation, the way she did when she was upset. "Don't give him anything. What the hell did he want?"

This was not quite the response Sanne was expecting from her sister.

"I think," Sanne said slowly, "he could tell that I was surprised, and that I might need to digest what he was saying. He said he'd call back later, after I'd had some time."

"What a bunch of bullshit," Marla replied. "This is exactly how it starts."

"How what starts? I'm lost."

"Oh, my dear, innocent sister. You do remember how you recently came into money, don't you?"

Which was how Sanne could afford to rent this rather fancy and certainly too-large house across from the land where the development was taking place. Compared to the one-room cabin Sanne had lived in before, tucked between two large brick buildings, her house was palatial.

It had been Della's idea. They had been at the old Mackenzie place, all ninety-seven acres of it. By then the land was graded, sewer and septic installed. Underfoot was a sidewalk, overhead a brand-new lamppost.

"I travel," Della had said. "You don't. One of us needs to be close by to make sure none of the contractors get confused and touch a single one of our trees."

Our trees.

Sanne smiled at the memory. Sanne's forest. Now Della's, too.

So now Sanne lived across Juniper Avenue from the village-to-be, and her beloved old growth forest.

This too-large house had kitchen counters you could camp on, if you liked marble. Against the wall was an entire section devoted to coffee—boxes, tins, and various complicated devices, most of which were housewarming gifts from Della, whose love language seemed to be presents.

Sanne's simple jar-and-chopstick brewing system was dwarfed by an elaborate espresso machine Della had given her. It gleamed silver on the black marble, glinting in light from the vaulted ceiling's high skylights.

Marla had also inherited money from Jerry, though not nearly as much. Sanne had objected, but Marla was fast to reassure: "Not only do you need it more," Marla had said matter-of-factly, "But Jerry owed you. I'm fine, sis. Chicago law firm partner—I make good bank. What Jerry left you is yours."

Sanne didn't like to think about it. It was a crazy amount.

"Your inheritance from Uncle Jerry," Marla prompted on the phone, her tone pedantic. "You remember, yes?"

Sanne clutched the phone tightly. "I remember."

"Listen to me," Marla said. "People are going to come out of the woodwork. Tell you all kinds of stories. Try to get under your skin, play on your kindness and care to see if you can be conned out of cash. Don't. Just don't."

"Don't what, exactly?"

"Anything with anyone who pulls on your heartstrings."

"So you think he's not our brother?"

Marla took an audible breath. "I'm not sure I care. Mom and

Dad married when she was twenty-two. They never hinted at another sibling. Frankly, I don't believe it. But even if it were true, it's incredibly suspicious timing. I call bullshit."

"All right. I'll be careful."

"Sure you will. You've got the heart and sense of a baby fawn. Don't answer his calls. Text him to talk to your lawyer. Give him my name and number."

Sanne reminded herself that this was Marla's way of showing love.

"Yes ma'am," Sanne said.

"That's better," Marla said, with a soft chuckle. "I love you, big sister."

Sanne was older by about a year. When they had been children, Sanne had often tried to protect Marla from—well, everything. Especially after their parents died.

But Marla hadn't needed the protection. As they matured, the age difference meant nothing, but it was still a tender joke between them that of the two, Marla fit more easily into the external world.

"Love you back," Sanne said. She looked around. "Hey. When are you coming to visit my strange, too-big house?"

"You've lived in hovels for as long as I can remember. This I have to see. Let me check my calendar and get back to you."

And then they were done.

Sanne brewed afternoon coffee, and considered tonight's lesson plan for the kids.

As she poured the hot water, her phone trilled.

Sanne took a moment, tuning into the caller, or at least the consequences of the call.

She could tell little, except that, whoever it was, whatever it was about, she was not going to have time for the coffee in front of her.

Sanne sighed, set down the kettle, and answered.

Rufus was new to public school, and there was a lot that he didn't know, but he had the strong impression that he was in trouble.

The principal's waiting room was very quiet, except for the ticking of the analog clock up on the wall, that seemed to Rufus to become louder and louder as the minutes passed, then an hour.

The four of them sat in chairs separated from each other, nearly at the four corners of the room, and had been sitting there for some time.

His ribs hurt where he'd been hit. Or elbowed. Or kicked. He wasn't sure. The four of them had been on the ground, and things got confusing. He wondered how bad his cheek looked where Nicholas had nailed him when Rufus had tried to get between him and Keyton, and Keyton had somehow swept Nicholas to the ground.

Across Nicholas's forehead was an oversized bandage. He looked back at Rufus with an expression that promised retribution.

Great. Only two months here, and Rufus already had an enemy.

Or maybe that wasn't what this was at all. Rufus knew that he could be a little dense about people sometimes, not always reading the non-verbals. That was a big part of why he liked hanging out with Angie and Keyton—he rarely needed to guess. They just told him.

But right now, looking around the room, he almost thought he could smell the stink of regret, that every one of them was thinking what they might have done differently if they had it to do over again.

For himself, Rufus thought it might have been better not to step in at all. If he'd known how hard Keyton could hit, he sure wouldn't have tried to protect zir.

Rufus touched his face, which was tender. An unused ice pack sat at the table to the side of his chair. But if Nicholas wasn't using his, Rufus sure wasn't going to.

At the far end of the room was a small desk at which sat a

woman. Her little name thing said she was Admin Maria Dyer. She wore a gray skirt and an ironed white buttoned-down blouse, a lot like how folks dressed at church.

They'd been here two hours already. Each of them had been privately interviewed, then returned to this room to sit, phones confiscated, forbidden by Ms. Dyer to talk to each other.

Or themselves, as Rufus found out, when he started to think about how he was going to explain this to his mother and realized he was saying the words out loud.

At first, Rufus had been thinking the three of them would still be able to make their evening session with Sanne. But as the wait dragged on, then Admin Maria Dyer walked over with a clipboard to each of them, quietly asking which of their parents they would prefer be called, Rufus realized with despair that the evening probably wouldn't include anything fun at all.

His father wasn't going to be at all happy about having to deal with this during his new job.

Dyer. Like "dire," Rufus thought glumly, wondering if she realized the message she was sending.

But then, when Ms. Dyer was talking with Angie, Rufus had his wacky and inspired idea.

Maybe he'd gotten used to wacky and wild things from this last year with Sanne and these two friends. Like saving the town of Marigold from demons. And knitting.

"Rufus?" Ms. Dyer asked, leaning close to show him her paper, which included the names and mobile numbers of his mother and father.

How to phrase it in a way that wasn't exactly a lie?

"You should call my governess," Rufus said, attempting to convey both confidence and boredom at the same time.

"Excuse me?" Ms. Dyer asked.

Rufus's English lit class had been reading Jane Eyre, and the word had stuck in his head. "Yes, she was going to mind me after school." *Mind me.* Not how kids talked, but if she asked, maybe he could sell it as how he was taught in homeschooling. "She's the one to call. Her name's Susanne Pascral." He recited Sanne's phone number, grateful that he had thought to memorize it.

Ms. Dyer's eyebrows rose, but she wrote down the number and took it with her into the principal's office.

Rufus met the shocked looks of Angie and Keyton with as placid an expression as he could manage. As he looked down and tried not to laugh, he reflected that maybe he wasn't as bad at reading other's faces as he'd thought.

"I see," Sanne said into the phone, which was not entirely true. "You say he's been in a fight, then?"

It was the word "governess" that did it. When school Admin Maria Dyer used it, with a tinge of unspoken skepticism in her voice, the part of Sanne that watched Masterpiece Theater kicked in.

What the bloody heck was Rufus doing?

Oh, Sanne knew perfectly well what he was doing. The kid was...well, he was invoking her. Sanne had done it herself a time or two with her mother when she'd gotten in trouble in elementary school.

Her mother had been a power, magically and socially, and there wasn't always a dividing line between the two. When her mother came to Sanne's elementary school to get Sanne out of whatever fix Sanne had gotten herself into, somehow things never turned out as badly as authorities implied.

The voice on the other end of the phone continued to describe Rufus's transgressions in a vague way, while the consequences the school was considering were perhaps needlessly specific.

Now Sanne could either rat Rufus out or step into her mother's formidable shoes and show up.

"I'll be right there," Sanne said, noting that part of her had decided while the rest of her was having a conversation about it.

Well, they were her kids. She taught them. Computers. More recently, craft work like weaving, knitting, and crocheting. And maybe some magic.

Their parents only paid for the first part. With any luck, the rest was still a secret.

Sanne padded in her wool socks to the front door, being careful on the slick, shiny dark wood. She considered for a long moment, and slid her feet into closed-toed brown leather shoes, ones she hardly ever wore. The sort an adult might wear.

The entryway had a mirror, and she looked herself over. Clearly she couldn't wear her usual comfortable, oversized jacket with all the right pockets.

Governess, eh?

She pawed through the hallway closet and pulled out a new and unworn beige jacket. Clean and unmarred by the scars of life, unlike Sanne's other clothes. Another gift from Della.

It belted, making Sanne look like someone who might not get kicked out of a PTA meeting. At least not until she began to speak.

Once outside, Sanne sat in her beat-up old dented black Nissan.

Terry, Della's husband, had urged Sanne to get a new car. Ideally a Mustang, like his.

Which made no sense, because her car was still working fine. Even better since she could afford to have it repaired. She patted the scratched and peeling dashboard with affection and drove to the Middle School.

She announced herself at the front desk, feeling entirely like an impostor.

Impostor governess? Impostor adult?

She was escorted into a room where the kids sat. She took a long look, taking in expression, posture, and energy currents.

Rufus was conflicted, but only a little more than usual. Angie looked like something had gotten under her skin and it hurt.

Keyton was struggling. She saw in Keyton's face the fear that begins to rise when a hot, defensive fury begins to wane, and one must look again at what happened.

All three of them looked at Sanne with what she read as desperation, as if she were a life raft.

So odd to be on this side of the line. Sanne vividly recalled one night of her senior year as she walked the silent corridors, classrooms, and auditorium of her high school, hearing only the soft brushes of her own boots. Into corners of classrooms and behind doorframes she had tucked small, scrolled papers on which she had penned spells in black and red ink. On each scroll she had drawn borders of green and violet flowers. Because if flowers weren't magic, what was?

Each scroll had a similar spell, intended to bring Chaos elements into the upcoming finals week. How else, she asked the air as she walked the halls that night, was she going to learn her craft, now that her mother was gone?

Sanne, the high school rebel, here at the principal's office to play the role of responsible adult. It was too funny.

Sanne didn't laugh.

Her gaze scanned to the other boy in the room. Taller than Rufus, he looked to be in a growth spurt. He was rubbing a shoulder. On his forehead was an oversized bandage.

Sanne looked more deeply, found the aftertaste of hot anger, the yang of masculine aggression. She sent a gentle, questing etheric touch toward him to see if he'd welcome it.

Back at her came a line of hot red-black something, edged with the feel and fleeting stench of necrotic flesh.

It wasn't an attack, so all Sanne needed to do was withdraw. It also wasn't anything she'd seen before.

Sanne cleared the space between them. The red-black energy retreated into the boy. He glared at her.

She struggled to keep the surprise from her face. You simply didn't see people carrying such swirls of power every day, let alone a boy his age. What was it?

Now that she was looking for it, Sanne saw flecks of that same strange red-black adhering to Angie, Keyton, and Rufus.

"Ms. Pascral?" At the far end of the room, a gray-skirted woman in a white blouse rose from her seat. "I'm the school admin, Maria Dyer," she said with an unsmiling expression. "Principal Hayes is ready to see you."

As Sanne followed the woman toward the imposingly closed door, some young part of her felt rising panic. Wasn't there some other adult here who could take this on?

With a subtle gesture, Sanne cast a quick calming spell into the space of the room, between the four children.

Then, for good measure, on herself, though it didn't seem to help.

She followed the woman into the principal's office.

CHAPTER

FIVE

The woman left, shutting the door behind Sanne with a rather decisive click.

In the sound, Sanne could feel the anxiety of tens of thousands of kids who had stood here before her. She swallowed.

The office was large, with unremarkable brown carpeting and pale yellow walls. At the center of the room a beat-up wooden desk from last century held a computer and various file folders neatly stacked. Black framed certificates lent an air of consequence. Through the window a tree-lined street below whispered songs of escape.

On bookshelves, sizable tomes seemed to promise wisdom on matters pedantic and profound.

At last she looked at the man standing behind the desk.

He grinned wide. "Sanne! What a surprise."

"Peter?" Sanne asked, incredulous. "You? You're the principal?"

Peter had a goatee, a neatly trimmed mustache, and a slightly receding hairline, all lightly salted with gray.

"Afraid so. I've risen to my level of incompetence. Now I can never get promoted."

It took Sanne a moment. She barked a surprised laugh.

"I can't tell you how many people don't get that joke," he said, "but I knew you would." he waved a hand at the door. "Of course, I can't say stuff like that to the staff." Peter's tone was warm. "Thanks for the laugh. I need it today."

He gestured her to the chair in front of him. They sat.

"I had no idea," Sanne said, looking around the room anew.

Peter gave a small, amused shrug. "You didn't ask us to talk about our jobs. You didn't even ask for last names."

Sanne recalled her wildcrafting class standing in a circle in the forest. Her prompt had been to describe a plant or tree that spoke to them. A few answered the question literally, which was always fun.

"And you, Sanne? In addition to teaching about plants, you're also a governess?"

His tone was gentle, but behind the words was the tone of someone used to getting answers.

Sanne took a breath. "Well. I do sometimes manage to govern them."

Peter's eyebrows rose. "Them?"

"Three of those kids in your waiting room. I tutor them. About computers." The other things she left unsaid.

Peter sat back in his chair, regarding her thoughtfully. "I see. You know them well?"

"I'd like to think so," Sanne answered cautiously.

Peter drummed his fingers on the desktop. "It's a challenging situation," he said. "Blows were exchanged, which is typically the line at which we do a suspension. But also some nasty words were exchanged. And there are extenuating circumstances."

"Like Rufus coming here from homeschooling?" Sanne asked.

"That's one, yes." He took a breath. "Nicholas's mother died suddenly, just a couple of months ago."

"Oh," said Sanne, feeling the words like a blow. "That's—" she exhaled slowly. "A very hard thing."

It certainly had been for Sanne and her sister Marla, eleven and ten, on one horrific New Year's Eve.

"On the plus side," Peter said, "no one disagrees about who threw the first blow, which simplifies things somewhat. But this qualifies as bullying behavior. And—it's happened before. I need —we need—to make sure it doesn't happen again."

Sanne's mind went to Angie. A single racist comment would explain her energetic signature. Maybe some gender-related slur had been directed at Keyton. Compassion filled her for the kids.

"I'm sure that whatever Nicholas said," Sanne replied, "he didn't mean. To lose your mother so suddenly is beyond wrenching, it's—"

"It wasn't Nicholas Gaffon." Peter's gaze on Sanne was steady.

"What? Oh." Sanne reassessed. "Rufus's family is fairly religious, and I've gotten the impression that they have some strong views. He's doing well in school, but surely still adjusting? A very different environment, public school and homeschooling."

"I have no doubt." Peter said. "But it's not Rufus, either, Sanne. From what I can tell, Rufus tried to stop this."

"What? Angie would never—"

"Keyton."

"Keyton?"

"Keyton."

Sanne sat back in her chair. "Oh."

"While Keyton is physically small by comparison to both of the boys, that doesn't excuse violent behavior. And there's Keyton's Jujitsu and MMA training."

"What?" Sanne asked.

"Keyton started training in fighting arts at nine years old. You're surprised?"

Sanne's vision of what had happened was shifting uncomfortably.

"Yes."

Peter drummed fingers again. "No one behaved well today. Your three tangled with each other, too. Not just Nicholas."

"Oh, hell," came out of Sanne's mouth.

A single nod from Peter. "I've seen you teach wildcrafting, and you're good. If these are your students, maybe you can encourage serious reflection about what happened. I've called Nicholas's father and was just about to call the other parents when you showed up. I can't let you take Rufus from school— you're not on the authorized list—governess or not. But I can delay my call to his parents, if you'd rather tell them yourself first."

"I would. Thank you."

Sanne had spoken with the Thompsons a few times when they'd come to pick Rufus up from sessions. They had treated her warmly, from which she concluded that they hadn't heard the rumors around the town that she was a witch.

"I am going to mandate an online anger management and anti-bullying class for all four. It's a three-day suspension. Do you think you could get your kids on board so the classes aren't a complete waste of time?"

It would help if Sanne could find out more about Nicholas and the red-black etheric stuff that was all over him. Was that from losing his mother? Sanne had seen her share of death, but had never seen this before.

Peter was watching her closely.

"I can try," she replied.

"That's a bit weak," Peter said, softening it with a small smile.

Sanne remembered the forest where she had met Peter and his wife, Donna, remembered how much they had both smiled that day.

"Look," Sanne said, "if I don't know what a plant is, I'm not going to tell you I do. I've worked with these kids for more than a year and never saw a trace of what you describe happening. I think there's something here beyond what meets the eye."

"Probably so," Peter replied. "But I'm not their therapist or softball coach. I've got a school to run. Let's make sure it doesn't happen again."

"I understand," Sanne said.

Peter stood with a polite, businesslike smile. Sanne stood with him. It was clear that the conversation was over.

His shoulders lowered with a small sigh. "If it does happen again, we'll be looking at more than a few days' suspension. I'm hoping you can work some of your best craft with them, Sanne."

Sanne knew that Peter meant wildcrafting, and meant it metaphorically.

But Sanne was thinking of her true craft. Her life's work.

Sanne returned to the waiting room. Nicholas was gone, presumably already picked up by his father.

Her three kids gave her a look of intensity.

"I'll call your parents," she said to them, nodding at Rufus. "Starting with yours."

"Will we still have class tonight?" asked Angie.

"I don't know," Sanne admitted.

"Oh, man," said Keyton, rocking back and forth in the chair.

"It'll be okay," Sanne said, instantly regretting the words. Weak magic, that, to say a thing when you weren't at all sure you could back it up. "Maybe," she added. From their faces, that didn't help.

It might not be okay. Suspensions were a big deal. They affected families.

And Rufus, who had been doing so well here—what if the Thompsons decided to pull him out of public school entirely and return him to homeschooling? Sanne knew that he didn't want that.

For that matter, what if the parents decided that Sanne was somehow the cause of what had happened, and ended their tutoring?

She found herself staring at the admin, who looked back. Could the woman tell that Sanne had no idea what she was doing?

Enough of that, she told herself sternly. She would simply go home and call the Thompsons. She'd say...what?

"Sanne, hey," Rufus said.

Sanne remembered a time when her mother stormed into a teacher's classroom after class to make her opinions known to the teacher, about homework with which her mother did not agree.

What would her mother have done now?

Sanne took a step toward the door that led into the hallway that would take her out of the building, which suddenly seemed like a great idea.

"Sanne, wait," Rufus said urgently. "Sanne?"

Rufus's voice finally broke through Sanne's haze.

The haze of fear. Simple fear. She was worried about losing the kids.

Sanne liked who she was with the kids. How parts of herself didn't have to hide when she was with them.

Rufus's eyes swiveled to the side, head immobile. Then he did it again, using his glance to point.

Sanne turned to look at the chair where Nicholas had sat. There, where cushion met seat-back, something glinted.

But Sanne couldn't just walk over. Maria Dyer was already watching her and Rufus suspiciously.

So she turned her back to Ms. Dyer and raised her eyebrows at her three kids.

Angie nodded slightly. She stood.

"Ms. Dyer?" Angie asked. "Is there a bathroom nearby? I'm so sorry, but it's my time of the month."

Angie gave Ms. Dyer a compelling yet vulnerable look, while behind her back she made a small gesture. Sanne felt the minor charm flow in the direction of the admin.

Sanne suppressed a proud smile. Angie, always the fast-thinking one.

Maria Dyer popped to her feet. "Oh, Angie," she said, coming around the desk. "You never need to apologize for your menses. Not to me, not to anyone. We've got a private bathroom down the hall with a code on it. I'll take you." Then, to Sanne, "Ms. Pascral? Can you stay a moment and watch them?"

"Of course," Sanne answered.

Angie and Dyer left together.

On the chair, half in the crack of the cushion, was a ring. Silver, maybe white gold, with an oval of night-blue star sapphire.

It must have belonged to Nicholas. She'd go back into Peter's office, and return it.

As she reached to pick it up, the ring gave her an energetic and offended spit, like a hissing cat.

A clear no. Sanne withdrew her hand.

"A talking ring," Sanne said, intrigued. She crouched down in front of the chair. "Hello, ring. Do you belong to Nicholas Gaffon?"

The return feeling was an unambiguous yes.

"All right," Sanne said. "I can take you to him, if you like."

Nicholas, the ring said.

"She's talking to it," Keyton whispered from behind her. "Wonder what it's saying."

"Wonder why my ribs still hurt," Rufus said. "Where you hit me."

"You shouldn't have gotten in my way."

"Wow."

"Hush," Sanne said over her shoulder. "Ring, I'll need to pick you up and hold you, put you in my pocket, so I can return you to Nicholas. Will you allow me to?"

The ring didn't answer, but judging by the ring-sized intensity wafting off of it, it was struggling with the question.

That gave Sanne an idea. She stood and reached into her beige coat pocket, pulling out an off-white silk pocket square, from a set Della had given her along with the coat, a scarf, and gloves—all top-quality, and all some shade of cream—all items Sanne would never wear.

She felt grateful to Della now.

Sanne crouched again, laying the pale handkerchief on the

seat next not touching the ring. "I could wrap you in that. Would that be okay?"

Nicholas.

"I'll do my best to return you to him," Sanne said. "provided that you mean him well, and take no action to bring him harm."

Sanne had never encountered a talking ring before, but she'd read enough fairy tales to know that making promises to enchanted items required one to exercise significant caution.

Also, her sister was a lawyer.

In the silence that followed, Sanne reflected that she was here talking to a piece of jewelry, while two of her kids sat behind her, their unresolved conflict thick in the air.

Well, she lived an unusual life.

Yes, the ring said at last.

Sanne wrapped the ring in the silk kerchief and stood, hand and ring in her pocket, just as Maria Dyer and Angie came back into the room.

"You ever need privacy, Angie, you come see, me okay?" said Maria Dyer.

"Thank you, Ms. Dyer," replied Angie with her best, most authentic smile.

Maria Dyer, Sanne decided, was all right.

Dyer looked over at Sanne. The smile left her face. "I've got this now, Ms. Pascral," she said firmly, in a tone that told Sanne that she was dismissed.

"I'll be going, then," Sanne said, slipping into governess-speak.

She paused at the door to make brief eye contact with the three kids, hoping to offer some encouragement and settled on what she hoped was a warm smile. They gave her weak smiles in return.

But the look the admin gave her made it clear her time was up.

"See you soon," she said to the three of them.

She hoped.

CHAPTER
SIX

Nicholas took a forkful of meatloaf and dipped it into a pool of ketchup at the side of his plate, hoping to make it seem like food. But it just sat there on his fork, in shades of brown and red.

He should be hungry by now, but his stomach was telling him that this was as much like food as a forkful of dirt. His appetite had been lousy these last two months.

At home, anyway. At school Nicholas inhaled everything on his cafeteria tray. Something about the sound of two-hundred kids chattering and yelling made his stomach recognize food.

Meatloaf. His mother used to make meatloaf.

He put the fork down on his plate.

And then there was the ring. He must have lost it the day of the fight—maybe even when he went to the ground, tripped by that wretched little monster, Keyton.

His mother had given him the ring on the last birthday he'd celebrated with her, when he turned thirteen. It had been hers, and it didn't fit him. But when she offered to get it resized, he'd refused. He wanted it just the way it was. So he carried it in his pocket.

A terrible decision. His mother's ring—the last thing she had given him—and now he'd lost it.

Just before the pain dragged him down the vortex, to a place where he couldn't breathe—that bleak cave of despair from which he was sure he'd never escape—some part of him shut it all down. Everything went flat.

Just a ring, after all.

As he'd walked from the car to the house after his father picked him up from school, he'd smelled rain coming, felt the quick breeze, and saw fast-moving clouds overhead.

On the ride back, he had wondered if his father would be upset about the suspension.

"Never mind that," was all his dad said, when Nicholas had told him.

Here at the table, hands in his lap, Nicholas listened for the wind to pick up outside. Because then, when the strange sounds came from upstairs, they could both blame it on a tree in the wind scraping the roof.

"You not eating?" his father asked, looking at Nicholas's plate.

"Not hungry," Nicholas replied.

"Okay."

No argument, even, and his dad didn't used to be like that. Would have, before his mother left, asked him questions, made him laugh, gotten him to eat another bite.

From upstairs, a thump, like someone dropping a book. Nicholas's breath caught. His father's expression froze.

"Damned maple tree," his father muttered. "Going to cut it back."

His father had said the same thing a week ago, during the last storm. When Nicholas had gone out the next day, he realized that didn't make any sense: no branches even touched the house.

Nicholas nodded anyway, surrendering to his father's story.

Overhead, a creaking sound, like something rolling across the floorboards.

For a moment their eyes met. Nicholas thought he saw something like fear flash across his father's face.

That couldn't be, because his dad had been a wilderness EMT

before Nicholas was born, an expert in avalanche rescue. Nicholas's mom and dad had met at an advanced aerial rescue training. His father didn't get afraid.

Another sound from upstairs, as if someone were knocking. His father's face went taut.

Blaming a tree was crazy. But if his father wasn't scared, neither was he.

"I'll go look," Nicholas said.

"No, I will," his dad said, and put his empty fork down, precisely, tines curved down over the edge of his plate, just as Nicholas's mother used to do.

Exactly as his mother used to do. Before she went, his father never did that.

Somehow the gesture caught Nicholas right in the gut. The aching hole in his chest came back, his eyes filled. Fortunately, his father was already standing, had turned, and didn't see.

His father slowly walked up the stairs. Nicholas heard his footsteps overhead, then nothing. Minutes passed. Nicholas thought he heard his father's voice.

Then his father descended the stairs, watching his feet as if they weren't to be trusted.

He sat again at the table. "It's nothing."

"But..." Nicholas began.

What could he say?

He wanted the sounds to be his mother, but he knew it wasn't, and anyway, that would be ridiculous. His mother had been a surgeon, a researcher, a scientist. It went without saying that science was real, and ghost stories were just stories. Ghosts didn't exist.

Nicholas remembered the hissing wind. The face that wasn't a face, yet somehow looked at him.

Imagination, nothing more.

"Okay," he replied. His father seemed frozen. "Dad?"

"Yeah." His father picked up his fork, then set it down again.

"I'm thinking, Nick," he said, not quite meeting Nicholas's eyes , "that we might sell the house."

Another gut punch. If they sold the house, then she really wasn't coming back. Nicholas froze where he sat.

After a while, his father stood, and they silently collected plates. His father saved the uneaten meal in a container to put in the fridge. Because it was what Nicholas's mother would have done.

Then his father went to his office and shut the door.

Nicholas walked the house, wondering why it seemed so small. Was this because of how fast he'd grown this last year? He passed the hallway of pictures, deliberately not looking, and came to his mother's office. He quietly tried the handle.

Still locked. Nicholas hadn't even known there was a key to this door until after EMS came to take his mother's body away, and he had gone there to find something of hers, anything, and the door wouldn't open.

For a few weeks after that, Nicholas assumed his father had locked it to keep things as they were, since the police had asked him to leave things untouched until they came back.

Then, a few days after his mother had been taken, a detective came and told Nicholas's father that the medical examiner had ruled his mother's death was from natural causes. Still the room stayed locked.

Ischemic stroke. The word came from the Greek *iskhaimos*, meaning to stop blood. Nicholas had looked it up, and now practiced saying it, like a mantra, as he walked to school.

His mother had been a neurosurgeon. She'd have wanted him to get her cause of death right. She had wanted him to go into medicine.

He walked the hallway. She used to stand right here, pausing to look at the pictures, calling him over. She'd smile, tell him the story behind each one, even when she'd already done it before. He remembered how he'd roll his eyes.

Now he'd give anything to hear her do it again.

For a moment, Nicholas let himself imagine she was here now. He looked at the picture of his parents' wedding, and imagined what she'd say. "What a day that was! My dad drank too much, but mom had him in her grip, of course." Another of Nicholas as a baby in a yellow onesie, grinning. "You were adorable. I couldn't believe I'd made you all by myself. With a little help." Nicholas at five on a tricycle. "Perpetual motion machine, hon."

A smaller, older black-and-white picture of her mom. Grandma Trinity had been a doctor of internal medicine and the only female doctor at her hospital. The frame was only four inches to a side, and showed Trinity Mallas as a young woman, in white lab coat, stethoscope around her neck, her expression something like smug.

His mother had been proud of her mom. They'd been close until Grandma Trinity died some six years ago. Grandma Trinity could be demanding—he remembered being sent upstairs to change out of grimy jeans that his parents wouldn't have even noticed.

But also she had given Nicholas the best presents. Like the magnetic marble run that had taken up most of his room that Christmas. That he still had.

Nicholas straightened Grandma Trinity's picture. His mother would want him to. Then he frowned, because it wasn't the first time he'd had to straighten this particular picture. Now that he thought about it, it had happened more than a few times.

He took the picture off the wall, checked the wire and hook. They both looked fine. He replaced the picture, making sure it was square.

CHAPTER

SEVEN

"He win?" asked the voice on the phone, that of Mr. Thompson.

"Excuse me?" Sanne replied.

"You said Rufus got into a fight. Did he win it?"

Sanne blinked, surprised, not quite sure how to answer. She stood at her kitchen sink, brushing stray coffee grounds into the sink. Rufus's father, judging by background traffic noise on the line, was at a construction site.

"Gave as good as he got," she said, thinking of the bruise on Rufus's face and frankly guessing.

Thompson grunted. "All right. Yeah, I'm happy to have you babysit him for this suspension. I've got to work every day, and his mom is busy helping his sister study for her SATs. Honestly, I don't think I want to see the anti-anger and bully management classes at all. Likely just piss me off. Thanks, Susanne. I appreciate it."

"Happy to," Sanne answered.

Next she called Angie's parents and then Keyton's. They each wanted their kids home that night, so the group tutoring session was off. However, they were happy to have Sanne take the kids for the suspension days and oversee their time away from school.

Sanne went into one of her two spare rooms, with most of her craft items. That meant boxes with skeins of colorful yarn and spools of thread and various other tools useful in textiles and woven works. But also books still packed, and her card decks and a few other items besides.

She'd set a few items on a narrow hallway table, almost certainly vintage mahogany—dark and scratched but loved—that she'd found at a local garage sale.

Even with her boxes in the corners, the room was nearly empty. It was mind-boggling to Sanne to have so much space.

On the narrow table was a flat slate stone, an irregular rectangle rough at the edges, but smooth and gray on the flat. Slate was a calm, harmonizing rock, one that didn't seek fast change, and rarely had strong opinions. A good place to set unresolved matters.

Next to it was a folded rectangle of silver-white silk velvet. Sanne laid the velvet on the slate, then took the kerchief-covered ring from her pocket, unwrapped it, and gently laid the ring on the velvet, taking care not to touch the ring directly.

"I'm going to try to find Nicholas," she told the ring. "Is there anything else you need? Anything else you would like to tell me?"

Along with the words, she sent a soothing wash of care toward the ring. But to Sanne's senses—at least at this moment—the silver metal with its pale six-pointed star sapphire stone didn't seem to be quite there.

She waited. The ring was silent. Almost as if it were just a ring.

Sanne left, closing the door quietly, and went into the kitchen to pop open her laptop to hunt for the Gaffon family.

She found a news article, a paragraph reporting the death of Gail Gaffon, Nicholas's mother, from a little over a month ago.

Gail Gaffon had been a neurosurgeon. Not exactly the sort of specialty you'd think to find in a small town like Marigold, but she worked in the city and called this small town home. She was survived by one child, Nicholas, and her husband, Matthew. As with most such announcements, it lacked any details. Like the cause of death.

An archive search revealed Matthew and Nicholas's deleted social media accounts, all about the time of Gail's death.

Strange. Usually people announced deaths on social media. Accepted condolences.

Finally, Sanne called Peter using the number he had provided years back for her wildcrafting class.

No answer. She was about to leave a voicemail, but thought better of it.

She needed to be careful about mentioning the ring. On the one hand, she wanted to return it to its owner, presumably Nicholas. On the other hand, the ring was some kind of aware, and Sanne dared not give it to an intermediary until she knew more.

That night in bed, Sanne heard something. It wasn't uncommon for Sanne to hear voices as she drifted off. Sometimes an energy force, or spirit from another realm, wanted to pass on a message. Or maybe just hear itself speak.

Other times the words were only the liminal ruminations of her own consciousness. Figuring out the difference was one of the most important parts of her craft.

As she slid into sleep, Sanne thought she heard singing.

***

At two in the morning, Sanne was certain.

She got up and walked toward the sound, which unsurprisingly was coming from her craft room.

She put an ear to the door and the sound stopped.

A singing sapphire ring. She smiled and slowly opened the door, stepping inside.

"Hello, ring," she said quietly. "Was that you? That was lovely."

No reply.

"How are you this early morning?"

Silence.

"Do you want to talk?" Sanne asked hopefully.

She stood there a long moment, long enough that some part of her started to question whether she'd heard it at all.

While stories about magic rings were a staple of literature going back centuries, to actually encounter a ring that spoke, and even sang—yes, she had truly heard it sing—was unusual even by the standards of Sanne's unusual life.

Puzzling, too. Perhaps the ring was like a scared animal, unexpectedly separated from its owner, and unwilling to engage with strangers.

What, she wondered, did the ring need?

Nicholas, that much was clear.

Sanne sighed softly, and backed out of the room, closing the door.

CHAPTER

EIGHT

The next morning the three kids showed up at Sanne's house, glum and sullen, laptops and backpacks slung over their shoulders. They plunked themselves down at the square kitchen table, audibly dropping bags to the floor.

Sanne winced. "Laptops don't like being banged about, folks."

"Neither do people," Rufus muttered sourly.

Angie stiffened. Keyton, still running on weary anger, looked away, lips pressed.

"And we're supposed to keep up on all our school work too?" asked Rufus. "How are we supposed to do that without even being in class?"

"You get email," Angie said, her tone flat. "It tells you what's due and when."

For even Angie to be in a bad mood told Sanne how tangled things were between the three of them. Sanne shifted her gaze to see deeper.

Bits of the odd red-black that came from Nicholas were still there on all three of them. Fading, but there.

Fading was a good direction, though. Was the red-black energy on Nicholas a result of the conflict?

43

Or had it caused it?

She looked them over. No one met her eyes. She let out a slow breath. Where to start?

With something else.

"I've got a problem," Sanne said, as she moved around the table, letting herself look as concerned as she felt. "I could use your help."

That got Sanne the dullest flickers of interest of the kids. Gazes slid around toward floors and walls.

Sanne waited. Silence was a powerful tool, a compelling force. Then she waited some more.

"What is it?" asked Angie finally, reluctantly, her curiosity winning the battle.

Sanne needed to find the Gaffon family, Nicholas in particular, and return his ring. She needed to talk to him to understand more about the strange red-black energy, so she could keep her kids clear of it, and hopefully the rest of the school as well.

But she let her gaze roam the room—a bit dramatically—and then came back to her students.

"Cookies," Sanne said.

Rufus looked up, lower jaw protruding as he considered. "You mean like browser cookies?"

Sanne kept a straight face, but did it in a way that made it obvious that she was struggling not to smile. She let the silence drag until all three of them were looking at her.

"We should be clearing our cookies so that no one is tracking us?" Angie guessed.

Keyton looked at the other two, for the first time, Sanne suspected, since the fight. "And there's three of us, and our laptops are often together, and we treat each other's devices like trusted sources, so...."

"So triangulation," Angie continued. "Man-in-the-middle attack. Privacy. Security. I bet Sanne knows of a specific threat."

Angie reached down to her feet and tugged out her laptop

from her bag, putting it on the table, and opening it. She began to type.

Rufus did likewise. Keyton scowled and, Sanne judged, not wanting to be left behind, followed suit.

Sanne waited.

A few minutes later Rufus shouted "Done!" raising both arms. He triumphantly closed his laptop.

Angie was a near-simultaneous second, shutting hers, and grinning, followed a minute later by a still-scowling Keyton.

"Gold stars all around," Sanne said to the contest that wasn't really a contest. "Good cyber hygiene, folks."

"But...?" asked Angie, watching Sanne closely, and clearly suspecting the other shoe was about to drop.

"But..." Sanne lengthened the word as she hammed up an expression of struggle, tilting her head side to side. "Oatmeal? Chocolate chip?"

Rufus groaned.

Keyton crossed zir arms.

"This was about actual cookies?" Angie asked. "What? Why?"

"For the construction crew across the way. Della told me to ply the crew with baked goods, because then they like you, and if they like you, they tell you what's going on at the site, and we want that. Since I'm here across the street with this enormous kitchen, and—finally!—some kitchen pixies to help me, I figured it was the perfect time. We've got a few hours before their lunchtime. Oatmeal? Chocolate chip?"

There was a clear answer.

"Both," said Rufus, finding it. "Oats are good for you, and every cookie should have chocolate. We want them to have energy to work."

So let's make it with good energy, Sanne thought, but kept that to herself. Sometimes words got in the way.

"How about double chocolate?" suggested Keyton.

"Triple," said Rufus.

"What does that even mean?" asked Angie.

"It means more chocolate," Sanne answered. "The multiplier is just a marketing trick."

"But the trick works," Rufus said. "No one pays attention to the oatmeal part once you've said 'triple chocolate'."

The other two nodded eagerly, and Sanne could feel the flow in the room shift a little. She helped it along a bit, cleaning up some of the dangling threads.

So they began. At Sanne's direction, they opened the fridge and cabinets and drawers, filling the huge center counter with butter, baking pans, and bags of flour.

"Where's the chocolate?" asked Rufus, and Sanne gestured. In moments, almost all the chocolate bars and tins of cacao powder Sanne owned were on the counter. The baking pans went onto the kitchen table.

The kids hadn't said much, but now Rufus wondered aloud how much chocolate was too much for it to be a cookie any more. Angie suggested that at that point, it would become a brownie. Keyton wondered if there was an equation that could describe a cookie, assuming chocolate as a variable. For a moment they all looked like they were about to abandon the cluttered counters for their laptops.

It was so charming that Sanne almost let them.

She clapped her hands and gave them a stern look.

"Cookies first," she said. "Math later."

"Yes, ma'am governess ma'am," said Rufus. The other two laughed—a balm to Sanne's heart.

The tension wasn't gone. There were still rips in the weave of their connection, bruised energetic knots all through each of them.

And bits of red-black.

Sanne could just about see Angie's emotional wound, even without knowing what it was. Rufus might be physically sore, but was clearly—and unsurprisingly—unsettled with Keyton. And Keyton—parts of Keyton were locked down, as if preparing for a storm.

Still work to do.

But first, cookies.

Sanne governed the baking process lightly, and only when she must. As the others worked, she spun silent spells to keep the room as clear of etheric tangles as she could, and to soothe what was possible to soothe.

The first batch went into the oven. The room began to fill with the rich, sweet baking scent of flour and vanilla and chocolate.

"Sanne," Angie said, "what about the classes we have to take?"

"And the homework," Keyton said, unsmiling.

"Wait," Rufus said. "What about the ring?"

"All in good time," Sanne said. "Let's get our cookies delivered, then I'll tell you what fun thing we're doing next."

Suspicious looks, but softer than when they'd first arrived. She'd bought them off. A bit. With cookies.

An old trick, but it worked.

The first batch was good enough that she had to stop them—and herself—from making it their second breakfast.

Sanne and the kids walked plates of oatmeal-chocolate-chocolate-and-chocolate cookies across Juniper Ave to where the crew in orange and yellow vests were sitting to eat lunch.

"Woah, hey, you can't—" called the foreman, a tall, lanky fellow with dreadlocks waving his arms. "Oh, it's you, Susanne. Hey. Careful there—we're still waiting on inspection before we fill it in."

Sanne and the kids walked around the open hole inside which were pipes and dirt.

"We brought you—" Keyton began, but as the crew surged forward it became clear that no one needed an explanation. In moments all of the crew had cookies in hand and mouth.

"Damn," said a woman with an open orange vest and a shirt that read "And I think to myself...what a wonderful weld."

"These are good," said a heavy-set fellow with an accent. "Where did you get them?"

"We *made* them," Rufus said, with obvious pride.

"You made these yourselves?" the foreman asked with clear surprise.

"I like the sidewalks," Angie said brightly. "Did you make them yourselves?"

The crew burst out laughing. "Okay, okay," said the foreman. "You made them. They're beautiful. But how'd you get them so perfectly round?"

"Oh, that! We used a round cookie cutter," Rufus said, holding his hands up in a circle to illustrate. "Each one, you put it around the baked cookie. Kind of shake it, until it's round. Has to be fresh out of the oven."

"Kind of how we trowel the sidewalks," said one of the crew.

"Rather eat these than sidewalk," said another, and everyone laughed.

After a few more minutes of this banter, at the moment when the conversation lagged, Sanne waved at the crew, and took the kids back to her house.

Time to try a different sort of nourishment.

Angie was annoyed with Keyton and trying not to show it.

After the cookie visit to the construction site, they had come back to Sanne's house and made sandwiches.

"We had dessert first!" Sanne had said, in that silly tone she sometimes used. They'd eaten sandwiches and a few more cookies.

Then, like ripping a bandaid off, Sanne had set up her wall-mounted TV and put on the online classes Principal Hayes had mandated, one after the other. In the breaks, she asked if anyone wanted to say what they thought, or how they were feeling.

No one did.

Angie actually found the classes interesting. She liked learning that there were ways to manage being mad, especially if you thought of it as something inside you, not outside you. She appreciated the pond analogy. Anger might be a fish, but you could be the pond.

She tried thinking of her annoyance with Keyton as a common carp swimming around inside the pond of Angie. It was a rather big fish.

But there was an even bigger fish inside, one she didn't want to look at.

The bullying class was harder to watch, with Keyton sitting right there, snorting and breathing, not able to admit any responsibility for the fight.

After the classes were over, Sanne took Rufus aside to another part of the house to chat, leaving Angie with Keyton.

Maybe Sanne thought Angie would talk some sense into Keyton. If so, Sanne was greatly mistaken; Angie had no plans to be nice to someone who couldn't admit to their own nastiness.

Maybe Angie should be annoyed at Sanne instead, for leaving her here with Keyton.

But she wasn't, and Sanne was being good to them—really good to them—and to their parents, by taking the three of them all day today—Friday, the first day of suspension—and then Monday and Tuesday as well.

Sanne had promised that if the three of them got caught up on their homework over the weekend, on Monday they could knit, or crochet, or visit the forest. Or all three.

Magic, in there somewhere, Angie hoped. The fun stuff.

But right now, Keyton was still being annoying.

"I don't care," Angie said sharply, as Keyton kept droning on, trying to show her something on zir laptop.

"Come on, Ang. This thing wasn't cheap."

"And we paid equal parts," Angie replied stiffly. "Please don't call me 'Ang'. I don't like it. At all."

"I'm sorry," Keyton said with what seemed to be genuine feeling, which softened Angie's irritation. Slightly.

Anyway, it wasn't Keyton who had said the thing in the fight that was the big fish swimming in the pond of Angie's feelings. And it wasn't so much what Rufus had said as how he'd said it.

She felt a catch in her throat, a tightness in her shoulders.

That one your girlfriend?

Hell, no!

Of course she wasn't his girlfriend. That was ridiculous. They were friends—or had been. That was all.

But he replied as if it would be a horrible, disgusting thing... Knowing what she knew about his family, his homeschooling, his church...she shouldn't be surprised.

She didn't like to think that her skin color made people—friends even—think about and treat her differently. But she should know better.

Hell, no!

Maybe it was time to move on from this tutoring group. Angie nearly always knew the answers to Sanne's questions before Keyton and Rufus did. Sometimes Angie delayed answering to give the others a chance.

Her parents would happily find her another tutor, if she asked. Maybe an online one. One with no other students.

At the thought, her heart felt heavy. But that's how it was, growing up. Or at least out-growing.

"Angie?" Keyton asked. "I said I was sorry."

"It's okay," Angie replied.

"It doesn't seem okay."

She almost let loose on Keyton right then and there. *Yeah? What about the stuff you said yesterday? Didn't you listen to the class we just had? I still have bruises on my arm where you hit me while you were having your little tantrum.*

Instead she shook her head slowly. "I'm fine." She gestured to the laptop. "What does this matter?"

"The weather rig was supposed to be pointing down, maybe a

20 degree angle, to shed water. Now it's pointing more like 45 degrees and to the side. Not where I left it."

"Maybe a bird moved it."

"Don't think so," Keyton said. "Shouldn't swivel so easily. I installed it. I don't think a bird could move it that much. Well, maybe an eagle. It was pointing at the lake. Now look."

The rig measured wind and light, but also barometric pressure and select pollutants. It had a small camera as part of the setup.

Angie looked, shrugged. "So? Where's that?"

Keyton shook zir head. "Don't know. Somewhere in town. That there is a roof."

Angie shrugged.

"I'm going to need to go back up and adjust it."

"What? Are you crazy?" Angie's voice dropped to an outraged whisper. "We're already in so much trouble. You especially."

"Not if we don't get caught."

Angie gaped at Keyton. "You started a fight at school. Any chance you remember that?"

"Nicholas Gaffon started it," Keyton said, zir eyes defocusing.

"Nope, nope," Angie said tightly. "I saw you throw the first punch."

"He called me a name."

Angie glared. "You do not get to hit people just because you don't like what they say. Unbelievable. If I did that, I'd be suspended for the rest of my damned life."

The intensity with which Angie spoke surprised even her.

Keyton cringed back a little.

Just then Sanne came in, smiling warmly. "Hey, Keyton, come with me? Talk a bit?"

"Sure," Keyton said, bouncing up from the couch, seeming eager to get away.

As if that weren't bad enough, now Rufus was here. Angie would be alone with him.

"I have to go to the bathroom," Angie announced, leaving the room.

There, in Sanne's fancy new bathroom, Angie stared at herself in the wide mirror. Her braids, her brown eyes, her dark skin, the maroon sweater. She shook her head and the beads at the ends of her locks brushed across her shoulders, and clattered together softly. A comforting sound.

She was smart. That she knew. She knew it because she often decided to hold back in class, or write a touch below her ability, so she didn't stand out, or get accused of plagiarism again. And her parents were smart, and had told her she was.

But they also said that she was pretty.

Hell, no.

Maybe they were wrong about that part. Or maybe she was only pretty to people with her skin color.

She reflected on the anger class, and the practice of saying what you were feeling—naming it.

In the mirror, Angie grimaced. "I'm angry," she said to her reflection. "Because I feel..."

She trailed off, turning her back on the mirror. She couldn't. Giving it voice was too much to bear.

CHAPTER
NINE

In the second of Sanne's three bedrooms—the one she was calling a guest room, though she hadn't had any guests yet—Sanne sat on the edge of the small bed, the one that used to be her only bed.

Keeping it had been a win in one of the friendly battles with Della, who had insisted on helping Sanne furnish this rental. Temporary lodgings, until her house in the development was built.

In Sanne's actual bedroom, a room as large as her entire one-room cabin had been before, there was a new bed—a huge new bed—clad with the high-count Egyptian cotton sheets that Della had insisted on.

At least they weren't beige. Sanne had won that round and slept on forest green sheets.

Sanne gestured Angie to a nearby, beat-up old green velvet loveseat, worn smooth by years, and flanked by stacks of cardboard boxes.

Who knew, maybe Sanne would have a guest in this room someday. Her sister kept threatening to visit, after all. But Marla was a big-city attorney. Partner now, too. Busy beyond belief.

Angie looked around at the boxes. "Still unpacking?"

"Not so much," admitted Sanne. "What's the point, if I'm moving again soon?"

Angie looked out the window and across Juniper Ave, toward the tree-lined construction, half-hidden behind Douglas fir and dogwood. "Be at least a year, you said."

"Yes."

Angie tapped a cardboard box. "I would think you might need whatever's in here, before then." Angie gave Sanne a questioning look. "And if you don't, why do you still have it?"

"You ask inconvenient questions, child," Sanne said with mock condescension, then laughed. "Maybe I want to surprise myself when I open them."

"Like with the box of demon eggs?" Angie asked with faux innocence.

Sanne gave a short exhale at this. "From my sister," Sanne said. "Who didn't know what was inside. And wouldn't believe it, even if she had. Maybe I'm just a packrat who can't bear to part with any of my trashy treasures."

Angie stared out the window again.

"How are you doing, Angie?" asked Sanne.

"Oh, I'm fine. Just fine."

Sanne gave the obviously false words a moment to breathe. The etheric space around Angie was compressed and tangled. Sanne worked the surface a bit to see if she could remove some of the red-black etheric stains.

"No, I'm not, not really," Angie said, then took a breath. "You know, I was just trying to get away from the crazy on the floor. Someone grabbed my ankle. I kicked to try to get free and there was a head or something and my toe still hurts. Then I stepped on someone, by accident, and fell on my ass." She shook her head, tone angry: "I don't know who they are."

Sanne understood Angie to mean Keyton and Rufus.

When Sanne had her conversation with Rufus, she managed to get most of the red-black goo off of him, and suspected that time would do the rest. But Angie—like Keyton—was helping maintain the clinging etheric stuff.

"I think you do know them," Sanne said gently. "But we each have many sides."

"I saw some sides I didn't like." Angie's tone was bitter.

"Maybe everyone has some fish swimming inside that they themselves can't see, and maybe even aren't entirely happy about."

Or maybe, Sanne thought, there was more to this than met the eye. The red-black energy was unlike anything she'd seen before.

As was the ring.

"Maybe," Angie said in a tortured tone.

Sanne wanted to take the girl in her arms and rock her and keep her safe from pain.

But no. Angie wasn't a girl. Angie's childhood was fading away. She faced the cliffs of adulthood.

Sanne's work as a teacher, if it was anything at all, was to give her kids the tools they needed to become the kind of adults they wanted to be. That meant letting them use the tools, and letting them walk on their own.

However wobbly their steps might be. However hard it might be to watch.

Speaking of tools...

Sanne went to the corner of the room and folded back the open flaps of a cardboard packing box. From it she removed a cedar box and opened it so Angie could see.

"Oh, lovely," Angie said of the stones. "What are they?"

"Various," Sanne answered of the stones, which ranged in color, shape, and texture. "Lapis, onyx, amber. Also tiger eye, hematite, calcite...That one is petrified wood. But those are just names. That doesn't tell what they are. Each has a feel, a perspective. A personality, if you will." Sanne set the box on a cardboard box at Angie's side. "I'd like to lend you a couple. Pick out any two that feel good to you."

Angie sorted through the stones with curiosity and pleasure, perhaps worth the exercise, all by itself.

Sanne watched how Angie's energy flowed with each stone. At last Angie selected two from the box. One black, one purple: a nugget of black rainbow obsidian, and a smooth orb of amethyst.

Sanne smiled at the choices, her heart easing. Angie would be all right.

"Take one in each hand," she said.

Angie held the amethyst out in her left hand, the obsidian in her right. "Which in which?"

"What feels like it fits best?" Sanne asked.

Angie considered, then swapped them.

This was an ancient diagnostic method for spirit healers, observing how a person chose and held stones. So this moment could tell Sanne the shape and texture of Angie's challenges and where her spirit might be able to go next.

If Sanne were any good at this, that was. Across the years, Sanne's work with stones had mostly been for herself.

First time for everything, she supposed.

But Sanne did know that each type of rock, and each individual specimen, carried with it various properties, offering different ways of seeing and changing.

In this case, the obsidian gave a pathway to recover from external influences. Amethyst could provide calm, clear-seeing. Both were adept at shifting from violence into compassion.

Perfect.

Angie stood and Sanne judged from her expression that she was taking a moment to see what they felt like. As Sanne watched, Angie's field shifted, the stones doing their work. More importantly, Angie was letting them, working with them, finding new balance.

The bits of sticky red-black on Angie faded and as her expression relaxed, her field brightened, and the stains vanished entirely.

Sanne exhaled surprise. It was one thing to clean another's

field—assuming you knew how, and it was possible—and another thing entirely to watch someone do it for themselves.

An elated flush went through Sanne. Angie had the knack. More than a knack, she could do the work, and could do it intuitively.

Rufus and Keyton had also shifted here in this room with Sanne and the stones they had chosen.

But not this fast, and not without help.

"What do I do now?" Angie asked, hands at her sides, the rocks within her curled fingers.

"Oh, Angie. You did it," Sanne said, allowing pride and joy into her voice. "You want to keep those two through the weekend?"

"Yes, please. Where did you get them?"

"I got the black obsidian from my mother, in the original set she gave me when I was nine. The amethyst..." Sanne took a breath. "The amethyst I found in my parents room, under my mother's pillow, the morning after New Year's Eve." Sanne trailed off for a moment. "The morning after they both died."

Sanne regretted the words the moment she'd said them.

Angie's mouth dropped open, her focus shifting to Sanne.

"It's okay," Sanne said.

"You never told us." Now Angie looked like she wanted to hug Sanne.

"It's been a lot of years. I'm fine. Just fine," Sanne said, aware, a moment too late, how her words echoed Angie's. "Angie, what you just did with the stones was impressive. See if you can do it again, over the weekend. Yeah?"

Angie smiled, a tentative yet genuine smile, the first Sanne had seen from her since before the fight. "Okay."

"Let's go back and join the others," Sanne said. Then, to Angie's expression: "You've got your stones. Remember what you did here. You can do it again."

"Okay."

Sanne considered the three teenagers in her living room.

Rufus and Keyton sat on the far ends of her dingy brown couch, the one Sanne had gotten on Buy Nothing Marigold, over Della's shocked objections. Angie perched in a chair, her stones in her hands.

They all looked better now, but there was still plenty of tension in the room.

Time to tell them.

"Let me tell you what I found out yesterday," Sanne said, "when I talked with your Principal Hayes. Nicholas's mother, Gail Gaffon, died suddenly a couple of months ago."

Judging by their expressions, they hadn't known, either.

Such a story would burn through a school, if anyone had known. Clearly Nicholas hadn't told anyone.

"How?" asked Rufus.

Sanne shook her head. "I couldn't find anything online about Gail Gaffon's cause of death."

"We could look," offered Angie.

"You could. But there's more."

"The ring," said Rufus.

Sanne nodded. "The ring. I think Nicholas accidentally dropped it on his seat in the waiting room. Now, it's asking for him. I'd like to return it. But I can't find any contact info for him or his father online, including social media—they deleted their accounts after Gail Gaffon died."

"Oh, man," said Keyton.

"So that's somewhere you could perhaps help."

"Yeah," Keyton said.

"But if you find something, it's for me. Don't contact them yourself. Okay?" The three of them nodded, looking eager to get to their laptops.

"There's more," Sanne said. How to tell them about the red-black etheric forces, when she herself wasn't sure what it was?

Well, adulthood. Uncertainty was part of the deal.

"When I came into the waiting room," Sanne said, "Nicholas had some rather powerful etheric...adhesion. Think slime or stain. I honestly don't know what it is. But some of it rubbed off on the three of you, possibly during the fight."

Angie stood abruptly, looking down at her magenta sweater and black leggings. Rufus had a look of worry as he rubbed his denim-clad knees.

But Keyton looked straight at Sanne with an expression that seemed to say *I knew something was odd.*

"The work we did in the other room," Sanne said with a nod at her guest room, "with the stones? That was, in part, to clean up what was attached to you. It's going away, but some of you still have it."

"I think," Keyton said hesitantly, "I can feel it."

"Good," Sanne said. "So let's consider: whatever you think caused this fight, whoever you hold responsible for hitting you—physically, verbally, or both—what are some other causes that might have gone into creating that fight?"

"Like Nicholas's mother's death," said Angie.

"Like that," Sanne agreed. "What else?"

"Not having social media," Rufus replied. "I know what that's like."

Sanne nodded.

"The etheric slime you mentioned," said Angie.

"Could be," Sanne said.

"Did someone cast a spell on him?" Keyton asked Sanne.

Sanne shrugged. "I don't know."

"The ring," said Rufus. "You said it's looking for him."

Angie cocked her head thoughtfully. "Do you know for sure that it's a good ring?"

Sanne shook her head. "I don't. But the ring, whatever it is, seems to me likely to be part of a fuller understanding of the event, too."

"I didn't know any of this," Keyton said, sounding annoyed.

"You couldn't," Sanne replied. "I didn't either. Principal Hayes was in my wildcrafting class a couple of years back, so he trusted me enough to tell me about Nicholas's mother. Let me ask you this: what other causes might have been at play in that fight, underneath the obvious ones, for each of *you*?"

"Like what, for example?" Rufus asked.

"Like..." Sanne said, "what made you step in between Keyton and Nicholas?"

"Well, I..." Rufus glanced sidelong at Keyton, who was glowering at no one in particular. Rufus looked down, fell silent.

There wasn't much trust in the room right now.

"Not asking you to answer," Sanne said gently. "I'm asking you to ask. You're at home for the weekend. Maybe ask the stones you selected. Let them help you reflect on the question."

Rufus pushed out his lower lip in the way he did when he was thinking. Angie nodded. Keyton grimaced.

A phone dinged.

"My mom's outside to pick me up," said Angie.

"Okay, folks," Sanne said. "You're with me Monday again. But if you need to talk before then, reach out."

Sanne walked to the dining area of the kitchen to watch the teens at the curbside waiting. They stood silently, as if they had nothing at all to say to each other.

Angie got into her mother's car. A bit later, Rufus piled into his father's forest green truck.

Keyton waited. After a bit, Sanne was about to go out and check, when Keyton strode off toward the bus stop.

CHAPTER

TEN

When Nicholas told his father about the required online classes, his dad just nodded, then left for his office. Before the door shut, Nicholas heard him start a show. An old sitcom from last century, judging by the music.

Nicholas skimmed a stream of animal vids. For a moment, somewhere between a tan puppy sliding down an incline into a pile of leaves and a black-and-white cat jumping onto the back of a golden retriever and refusing to get off the dog who was spinning, Nicholas managed to forget.

The good thing about forgetting was that you could almost imagine life as it used to be.

The bad thing was remembering again.

He slumped on the couch and stared at nothing, trying to make sense of what had happened.

It was early March that it had started. His mother said she wasn't feeling well. Then there were a bunch of tests. The diagnosis had come back with brain cancer.

She assured Nicholas that the prognosis was good, not to worry. There'd be a surgery. See what they'd find. Maybe radiation. It was simply something to take care of.

She was a doctor. A neurosurgeon, of all things. Her matter-of-fact tone and optimism convinced Nicholas.

But the surgery didn't fix it.

Nothing to worry about, she said; the radiation would.

When Nicholas thought about it later, he felt like a fool. The signs were all there. She stopped going to work. She spent more time with Nicholas than ever before. She tired quickly.

They had sat on this couch, right here and talked about plans for the future.

Then, on the night of August 18th, she didn't come out of her room for dinner. His father said that she wasn't feeling well.

No, Nicholas couldn't see her. Let her rest.

Nicholas ate alone. Played games. Quietly, so he could hear if anything happened. If they needed him.

The next morning, when his father came out of their room, Nicholas asked how she was.

His father wouldn't answer.

Nicholas asked again. Got more insistent.

Let her be, his father yelled. *You want her to get better, don't you?*

His father didn't yell.

Nicholas backed away. Told himself that his father was an EMT. Knew knew what he was doing. Would send for a doctor if she needed it.

The day wore on minute by minute, in a grinding silence, the house tight and small and oppressive. Nicholas didn't dare leave, in case she needed him.

Later, when his father came out and went downstairs, Nicholas tried the door of his parent's room.

Locked. Another door he didn't realize had a key.

"Mom?" he asked through the keyhole. "Mom?" Then, louder, as loud as he dared: "Mom!"

His father came back upstairs and Nicholas slunk back from the door, down the hall to his room.

"She'll be fine," his father said to him. Or to himself.

That night, Nicholas lay in bed, his imagination leading him to horrible places. Something was wrong. He just didn't know what.

Then, at 11:27am, the police came. They talked to his father in another room and Nicholas couldn't make it out.

The EMTs came and took Nicholas's mother away, on a stretcher, all covered.

Just like that, it was over.

His mother had told him it would be okay. It wasn't okay.

"It can happen that fast," his mother's brother Roland told him later, on the phone. Roland was a physician's assistant. "If you need anything, Nicholas, anything at all…"

What to say to that? The one thing he needed, he couldn't have: his mother back.

Now, sitting on the couch, Nicholas realized that animal vids were still playing on his phone. He stopped the vids, set the phone down on the glass coffee table, took the remote, and turned on the big screen, following the links to the online classes.

"What's the point?" he asked the empty room. "Why should I care?"

He knew what his mother would say to that: *Hon, you hit someone. Least you can do is try to understand why.*

"This class is probably crap," he replied.

I hope it is, came a different voice from inside his head. *You'll learn more. If the class is quality, you learn the material. If it's not, you study the teacher and their approach—or lack thereof. What is effective? What fails? Study, child. Study and learn.*

Nicholas sat up straight, his breath coming fast. Is this what grief did, made you hear people who weren't there?

"Grandma?" he whispered.

No reply.

Nicholas leaned back on the couch. What did he really know? What was he sure of?

Not much, not since she left.

Another ten minutes. Twenty. He was still holding the remote.

He cued the first class, entered his school-supplied code, and sat back to watch.

When both videos were done, he reflected that they weren't nearly as bad as he'd expected. He liked the part about the pond and the fish. Kind of reminded him of a children's book he had, about a whale, that Grandma Trinity had given him when he was five.

He went upstairs, locked his door, and went to his bookcases. Each one was overstuffed, books filling every gap vertical and horizontal. That was because he never got rid of any, and that was because he could never quite figure out what books he wouldn't want to read again.

The one about the whale, for example. Now that he couldn't find it, he wanted it even more.

He stopped looking for a bit, ending up re-reading *The Hobbit*. For a time he was somewhere else, somewhere that his mother hadn't died and his father hadn't become a stranger.

He returned to the search. Two hours later, piles of books filled the green-yellow-striped carpet like half-built fortress towers.

There it was, the picture book. He opened the cover, read the inscription on the inside of the front cover:

For my clever grandson. Love, Grandma.

Even after all that work to find it, that was as much as he could read, what with his vision going fuzzy as his eyes filled.

He climbed into bed fully clothed, hugging the book to his chest.

ELEVEN

In the small hours of the night Sanne woke to soft singing. Clad in her pajamas, she made her way to the ring.

The guest room was shadow on shadow, a dim light through the window from a moon behind clouds.

The singing stopped as Sanne arrived.

Sanne crossed her legs and let herself down to sit on the carpet, the ring at about her eye level. For a time, she simply sat, feeling the quiet, tender energy in the room.

"My name is Sanne," she said at last. "Short for Susanne. My parents named me for a famous song by Leonard Cohen. They played it for me starting when I was a toddler. But little me, I only made out the second syllable, so that's what I thought my name was: Sanne."

She paused to see if the ring had anything to say. It didn't. She continued.

"I asked them: why doesn't my name have the Z-spelling, like the woman in the song? Every time, I'd get a different answer. As I grew up, I began to suspect that it had been a simple mistake, that in the frenzy of giving birth to their first child—me—they spelled the name the first way it came to them.

"One day, out of the blue, my mother said: 'Baby, you take

that Z-spelling any time you want.' For years, every birthday, I'd think: maybe this year. But then..."

Sanne exhaled, surprised to find her eyes stinging. She glanced at the ring, and felt—or perhaps imagined—that it was listening attentively.

"But then, one night, my parents' car was hit by a drunk driver. They died. After that, I wasn't going to change my name. It was one of the few things they'd given me that I had left."

Nicholas, said the ring, a soft lament.

At that moment, Sanne became certain: the ring was Gail Gaffon. Or some part of her.

"I'm trying," Sanne told the ring, wiping tears from her face. "I swear I'll get you to him, if I possibly can. Is there anything else that you need, or that I can do?"

The ring was silent.

"What you were singing," Sanne said, when she felt sure the ring wasn't going to reply. "Sounded a little like my song. That's how it woke me, and why I came in. My mother used to sing to me."

Sanne felt sad, then deeply sad. She wasn't sure how much of the sorrow was hers, and how much was the ring's.

Both, perhaps.

"Would you like me to stay?" Sanne asked.

Again, no answer.

Well, sometimes you just had to step in and find out.

From the closet Sanne took a mat and sleeping bag and pillow, laid it out north-south, near but not too near the ring.

She sat on the bedroll, clearing her own space. Making an opening.

Sometimes listening was the greatest magic.

At last, Sanne snuggled into the bag, fluffing the pillow under her head. She thought of her mother and father and the gifts they had left her.

Her mother gave her a doorway into the etheric world, with

the bridge of spellcraft, and taught her how to distinguish between what was true and what was imagination.

Her father gave her a methodology to explore the world from many angles, inspiring Sanne to see the world without bias whenever she could manage it.

And both of them gave her love.

As Sanne drifted off, the ring began to sing again, so quietly that it wove through Sanne's dreams. A lullaby, the sort of spell a mother might use to sing a child to sleep.

Sanne slept.

CHAPTER

TWELVE

Nicholas turned his gaze from his phone to the ceiling. It was five minutes past six on Saturday morning, and he was wide awake.

He took inventory of the things he was sure about, and the things he wasn't. There wasn't much in the former category.

A terrible question had woken him, and now he was done sleeping.

He got out of bed, dressed in yesterday's shirt, jeans, and dirty white socks, and padded the halls of the house that, until two months ago, had been home.

In the shadowy light of pre-dawn, he went to the living room, and then the kitchen. In the living room, he took in the pale blue couch and the wood coffee table. A painting hung on the wall of a pale figure, dancing.

In the kitchen, the chairs with burgundy pillows, the dark wood table, a red and white ceramic mug by the edge of the white counter.

He tried to see each thing as it had been before his mother had died. Then again, as it was now.

Worlds apart, the two houses, but the difference told him nothing.

He walked the hallways.

Only now did he let himself put words to the haunting question: what had his father done?

Had Matthew Gaffon—Nicholas felt the need to call his father by his full name, because in the face of that question he could not bear to think of him as his father—done something, or failed to do something, that ended his mother's life?

Inside Nicholas, a lump like blackened coal, a hardness that had been there since her death. He felt it warm, as if from a nearby flame.

Grief makes you kind of weird, Nicholas reflected. Like right now, he found the heat of his anger welcome.

For sure, it was better than agony. Almost anything was. Like when that little creep Keyton had swept him off his feet, crashing Nicholas to the floor. He still hurt—head, arm, and a few other places besides. In that moment, everything had become clear.

It got little less clear afterward, in the principal's office, when Mr. Hayes told Nicholas he was in trouble for hitting back.

But that didn't matter. The important thing was finding out what was true.

Fact was, Matthew Gaffon was nothing like the father Nicholas had known. His face, when he looked at Nicholas at all, didn't move. His words, when he used any, were empty. Nicholas might as well have been a chair.

The medical examiner's report had said natural causes.

But it also said that Gail Gaffon died on August 18th, not August 20th, when Nicholas saw her leave home for good. What was Nicholas supposed to believe?

Nicholas passed the hallway of pictures. He paused. Grandma Trinity's picture was askew.

He adjusted it, hissing: "Stop it, Grandma. I don't have time for this."

For some reason, saying that out loud, caught him somewhere deep. Nicholas put a hand to the wall, his forehead to his hand, and for a minute sobbed silently.

Then cut it off. He couldn't, not now. He had a job to do. All the imaginary voices and skewed pictures in the world weren't going to do it for him.

He looked at the pictures in the dim hallway, not seeing them.

He had to get answers. He had to get out of this damned house. Do some thinking. Figure out how to avenge his mother's death.

CHAPTER

THIRTEEN

"Did I wake you?" Keyton asked with an innocent expression.

Keyton stood outside Sanne's door on the front steps, hands in pockets of a faded blue hoodie that would have been nothing like warm enough for Sanne this cool, foggy morning.

Sanne stood in striped robe and flannel PJs, swaying slightly, blinking, trying to wake up and not feeling much like she was succeeding.

She did, however, understand Keyton's tone of voice. It said, I know I did, but can we pretend that I didn't realize how early it was and it was an honest mistake?

What was it, seven o'clock? Eight? Sanne glanced at the digital clock just visible in the other room.

Seven. By the Fates....

"Were we supposed to meet?" she asked, appalled at the thought that her past self might have scheduled something this early without leaving her a note.

"You said," Keyton replied, "if we needed to talk, to reach out."

Sanne nodded slowly, taking this in. "I thought you might text or email."

Keyton bounced a little, glancing to either side. The street was empty. "Well, yeah. But I figured if I showed up..." Keyton shrugged.

Sanne was cold. "Come in," she said, standing aside.

Keyton strode into the living room and Sanne shut the door. Keyton stared up at the skylights.

"If you showed up...?" Sanne prompted.

Keyton let zir shoulder pack slide to the floor, then opened a hand, revealing a rock, the one Sanne had lent. Keyton had been the only one of the three who had only taken one rock.

"I couldn't sleep," Keyton said, pulling out the white crystalline rock, shot through with green and magenta.

"Go on," Sanne said, taking a few steps toward the kitchen, her mind on coffee.

"Thing is...look," Keyton said urgently, holding it up.

Sanne turned, slightly exasperated. It was her stone, after all. She'd had it for years. She knew what it looked like.

Ah, the trap: as soon as you were sure you knew a thing, you stopped looking. So she stepped closer, trying to see it anew.

The rock was marbled with thick lines and splotches of green and magenta, called watermelon tourmaline. Some folks in the energy-stone world also called it the bridge stone, for its ability to connect different world views. To heal rifts.

"What am I looking for?" she asked.

Keyton's face dropped. "Never mind." Keyton's fingers closed around the rock, making a fist.

"Stop that," Sanne snapped, too groggy to speak with more grace. "There are lots of ways to look at things, and I am not all-seeing. Especially not before coffee. Come on, show me again."

Keyton gave a teenager's sigh, and held open zir palm.

"Ah," Sanne said slowly. "It's got some red-black on it.

"Yeah! Thought so," Keyton replied, instantly brightening. "But how?"

"Well...you," Sanne said, shifting her vision to see Keyton's energy field. "You're carrying it. Reinforcing it. Even though I'm pretty sure it didn't start with you." She made a thoughtful sound. "Hang on."

Sanne went into her guest room, and brought back a flat disk of white selenite stone, some four inches in diameter. She set the selenite disk on the kitchen table.

"Put the rock on there," she said. Keyton did. "Give it a few minutes, and we'll see what it does. And let me make some coffee."

Sanne went to the coffee counter as if drawn, half on auto-autopilot.

No, wait. She forced herself to take a deep breath, and as she exhaled, she breathed out a spell of clarity and harmony, one she had learned not from her mother, but her father.

I don't believe any of this woo stuff, he had said to eight-year-old Sanne. *But when I hum this, I get along with your mother better, so...* He shrugged and smiled.

Sanne had memorized it.

The words were simple:

> Look to see
> Listen to hear
> Come with me
> Near and dear

Sanne poured grounds into a gold-plated cone and hot water from the glass kettle—another expensive device Della had gotten for her, which warmed itself on a schedule. Steam rose from the cone, the rich scent of coffee filled her nose.

"Get you something?" Sanne asked Keyton.

"No, thanks." Keyton took out the laptop from the pack, popping it up on the glass coffee table, and kneeling on the floor to type.

Sanne wrapped her hands around the glass mug.

Sometimes, especially when she was groggy, she worked to slow herself down, to feel into the moment. This moment, in which a dribble of dark brew trailed invitingly into her clear glass mug.

Where had it come from? Sanne sensed into the origin, finding the wet, rich warm lands of South America. There she felt the presence of those who cultivate coffee trees, who pick the ripe, deep red coffee cherries. In flashes she saw the many who sort and load sacks of beans onto wagons, then later onto train, ship, and truck.

Hundreds, easily, whose labor and care, blood and sweat, made it possible for Sanne to have this single cup of fine brew.

Sanne exhaled a blessing to all who brought her this gift, with special gratitude to those who spoke to the plants directly, whose thought and care brought forth an interlocking community of life that grew from healthy soil.

She sipped. It was so good.

"See," Keyton said, gesturing at the laptop. "It's not pointing how I left it, toward cloud cover. Angie said maybe it slipped, but that makes exactly no sense, because it was firmly attached when I put it up there. She—"

"Up where?" Sanne asked, walking around the counter into the living room to see Keyton's screen.

"—she thought maybe a bird, but no, I said, unless it's an eagle. They only weigh ten or fifteen pounds, but did you know they can lift things heavier than they are? They can have wingspans as much as eight feet. Ever seen them fight? Grab, then windmill? It's amazing. Anyway, up on the pole, the camera's pointing—"

"Keyton," Sanne said. "What pole?"

Keyton poked a finger at the screen. "—pointing at a rooftop. I wondered where that was, figuring it was weirdly random, but actually—"

"Keyton, hang on."

"Would you just let me finish?" Keyton shouted.

So much for clarity and harmony, Sanne thought wryly.

Or maybe sometimes, the spell just didn't take as well as you thought.

Sanne let her vision go wide. She cleared some of the anger from the space, then took another sip of brew, giving Keyton a mild and curious look—an invitation to continue.

"That roof, in the background?" Keyton continued. "See the glint? That's solar. So last night I looked up the town solar panel permits, cross referenced it with google street view and home sales. That house, it turns out, is right next door to guess who? Someone named Matthew Gaffon."

Keyton stood, giving Sanne a triumphant grin.

"Well, well. Good job," Sanne said.

Keyton bowed. "Thank you."

Sanne walked to the kitchen table. There, the selenite disk had cleared the magenta and green tourmaline of the red-black smudges.

"Your stone's clean," Sanne said.

Keyton joined her, fingers spread, reached out to take the rock, then stopped midair. "I don't want to corrupt it again."

Sanne set her glass mug on the table. "Then don't."

"What do you mean?"

Sanne sat at the table, regarding the green-and-magenta tourmaline, carefully not looking at Keyton. Not yet.

"You know what the red-black stuff feels like when it's on you. And you also felt it on the stone."

Keyton nodded. "I think so."

"You can learn to clear it off yourself, though first you have to decide if you want to. You can learn to hold it within your field. The red-black energy didn't start with you, but it's yours now. You can decide how it goes out into the world. If it does."

"I can?"

"This is somewhat more advanced work." At last Sanne looked at Keyton, giving zir a look that she hoped conveyed, *of course you can.* "Start with the intention to keep the red-black contained in your space. You feel it, after all. Can you keep the parts of you that touch the stone clear of it? Or, if not clear, tell the red-black whatever-it-is to stay with you?"

"Maybe?" Keyton's gaze refocused. As Sanne watched, the red-black smudges on Keyton tightened and flattened.

Sanne smiled. "Yes. Like that."

Keyton reached for the stone, hesitating again, then decisively took it in hand and held it high, expression full of concentration.

"Am I doing it?"

"You are," Sanne said.

Keyton beamed, slowly putting the stone in zir pants pocket.

"This is foundational for bigger workings," Sanne said, "to learn how to direct power. To contain it when you must. You don't want it running around loose, after all."

"Like the demons we trapped?"

"Like that."

"I was thinking of those eggs, actually," Keyton said. "As if I could put that sort of shell around it, in just the right place."

"Yes," Sanne said, pleased.

Keyton grinned, the first truly happy expression Sanne had seen from Keyton since before the fight.

"Okay," Keyton said. "Let's go."

"Go?"

"To the Gaffon house. To return the ring."

Sanne stood, taking her now-empty glass mug to the sink. She set it on the white porcelain, considering how to reply, then turned toward Keyton.

"It would be better, I think, if I went by myself. Okay?"

Keyton shrugged. "Sure." Keyton pulled out zir phone, fiddled. Sanne heard her own phone chime. She picked it up from the counter. Sure enough, an address. A bit of a walk from here, but she could use one anyway.

"Don't know what I'll find there," Sanne said. "So best I go without you, this time. Next time, who knows."

"I said fine."

Yes, but not like you meant it, Sanne thought.

"Shall I walk you to the bus stop?" Sanne asked.

Keyton shrugged, put zir laptop in the backpack, swung it over a shoulder, and walked to the door, waiting.

Sanne went to her room, dressed. In the craft room, she wrapped the ring in the silk pocket square, putting it in her left pants pocket. Then the guest room, where Sanne selected three stones and put them in her right.

Grabbing a coat and phone, she tugged on short, brown boots, and joined Keyton. Outside, they walked to Juniper Ave, where Keyton paused at the crosswalk to cross. Not the direction of the bus stop.

"Going to see the trees," Keyton said flatly.

"Good idea," Sanne said.

"Yeah? Will you come?" Keyton's tone was suddenly raw, vulnerable.

"Gladly," Sanne replied.

The ring could wait a little bit. She patted her pocket, and felt the metal of the band.

Together, she and Keyton went into the forest.

They walked an animal trail that threaded around maple, fir, alder, and cedar, and was lined with sword fern, wild rose, salal, and the occasional nursery stump hosting plant, insect, and fungi.

Sanne inhaled the forest air—good medicine all by itself— filled with late-season flowers, rotting leaves, and all manner of richness from damp loam and mushrooms.

They reached the clearing. There, the three great trees with their brown, corded pillars rose into evergreen branches holding the sky.

May we approach? she asked the three ancient creatures.

The answer was a welcoming whisper. Sanne tasted dirt and leaf and the knowledge of centuries.

She always felt young here. Leaning into the feeling, she

sensed the generational time of trees, deep roots underfoot, high branches taking in the sun. She picked her way through the thick loam, stepping around the occasional moss-covered rock.

Then she realized Keyton was not with her. She turned. Keyton was sitting on the ground, at what Sanne thought of as the outer ring. It was the limit of the root system, the drip-line, the extent of canopy fingertips.

Keyton was hunched over, head in hands.

Sanne walked back and crouched down. "Keyton?"

In a small voice Keyton asked: "Am I going to be angry forever?"

Sanne sat, heedless of the damp soaking through her jeans, and reflected on the lecture she'd given to the three kids only the day before.

Other underlying causes, not so obvious.

She'd missed something with Keyton. That, at least, was now obvious. The clues were there: waiting outside for a ride that didn't come. Arriving at her place early on a weekend morning.

"I'm impressed," Sanne said with a gentle smile.

Keyton looked up, met her gaze, face showing surprise. "What?"

"Two things," Sanne replied. "You just spoke about your anger as though it's inside you, rather than you inside it. No small thing. And also, it sounds like you might not want to feel it forever, a choice that not everyone can make. Those are adult moves."

Keyton considered. "Like the pond and the fish. If my anger is the pond, instead of me, then I'm only a fish."

"Like that." Sanne could feel the trees behind her, could feel their regard in the air. The shift in Keyton, sitting on the ground, was being helped.

"You said I was reinforcing the stuff on me that I got in the fight. What if I wanted to get rid of it? Completely?"

Sanne nodded. "Let me ask you this: if you could do anything at all to express that anger, what would it be? No judgment—anything."

"See, that's the thing," Keyton said, immediately animated. "I had him, right there on the ground, totally open for the perfect kick. Then someone—Angie, I think—kicked me in the head. By accident. You ask what I'd do? I'd kick that bastard in the balls, which is what he deserved after what he called me."

"You'd hit him back, then."

"Hard."

"And what would you want him to do in response? Ideally. Perfect world."

"Perfect? Grovel. Apologize."

Sanne nodded. "So let's say he does. 'Sorry I called you—' whatever it was. You've got your apology. Feel all better?"

Keyton considered. "Maybe."

Sanne grinned. "Let's try this: what if he didn't just apologize. He understood how you felt. Really got how it hurt you when he said what he said. And you were certain. And then he apologized."

"Yeah. That would be better."

"So hitting him is just you settling for what you think you can get. The real win is having him feel what you felt."

"But that'll never happen."

"You can't know that, though. But if you really want to get over the anger, now's the point where you level up even further. Given all that you know or can guess, you try to understand how he might have felt, too."

For a long moment neither spoke. A squirrel scraped its way up the trunk of a tree. A sparrow chirruped.

Keyton reached into a pocket and brought out the tourmaline.

"Don't know if I'm ready for that," Keyton muttered.

"Impressed again," Sanne said.

"What now?" Keyton asked with a small, self-conscious grin.

"To see something, but know that you're not ready for it—

and own that—that's something very few adults can do. You just did it."

"Cool," Keyton said. Sanne saw the red-black goo on Keyton fade. It wasn't gone, but Sanne suspected that Keyton now had it on the run.

"I should go home," Keyton said, a weight to the tone.

"You want a ride?"

"I think I'll walk."

What's going on at home, Keyton? Sanne thought, but decided not to ask. This had been enough. "I'm here if you want to talk. Any time."

They stood, and stood for another ten minutes, just breathing together. Keyton kept looking at the center tree, and seemed to be considering going there, but instead gripped the stone. The red-black smudges faded more.

"Thanks," Keyton said at last.

CHAPTER

FOURTEEN

Nicholas felt a bit clearer-headed when he left the house, enough to realize that there wasn't much in the way of fact-finding he could do on a Saturday.

Or any day, being thirteen. It wasn't as if he could just walk into the town's medical examiner's office and demand answers. He doubted they'd even talk to him. Maybe his father had told them not to—he was in EMS, after all.

It had rained lightly. He could smell the wetness of plants and earth, and could feel the coolness of the early morning on his face.

He strode past new townhouses and old bungalows—white, pink, pale blue, brown—blurs in his peripheral vision as he stared down at the sidewalk. He looked up long enough at the corner to make sure there were no cars and kept going.

When his mind began to turn to the unanswerable and the unbearable, he jogged, leaping over sidewalk cracks and skirting piles of wet leaves.

When that didn't stop the chattering in his mind, he ran full out, the swelling on his shin and bruises on chest and arms from the fight hurting hot.

It was good. The hurt. The run. It cleared his mind. So he did it again, block after block.

At last he slowed, bent over, gulped air, and walked on.

How trapped he had been these last months at home, his thoughts like mice in iron tunnels, helpless to escape, unable to chew through.

Now he had air. He looked up. Clouds. The pale of morning, hinting at sun later.

His walk took him toward Main Street, but no—too many people. He doubled back, jogging again, heading toward the green space of the hill and copper-green water tower.

The tower was one hundred and twenty feet high. He'd looked it up when he was eight, told his mother that he wanted to go to the top. His mother had said—

No.

He tossed that memory into the dark cave.

One time, about two years ago, he had started to climb this tower, but had come down quickly, afraid of the height.

He wasn't afraid any more.

The hill was mowed grass, except around the wide base of the green tower, where the bulbous tank's eight legs sank into concrete.

A harder fall, Nicholas thought wryly.

But no, he had no intention of falling. He just wanted to get up, to see what he could see. Give his thoughts room to think.

He launched himself at the heavy metal lattice on the nearest leg, and heaved himself upward.

It was easier this time. He'd grown—a lot, according to his parents. Last June, on his birthday, his mother had put him to stand at the doorjamb where they marked his height, and she said, *Nicholas, you—*

No, no. Into the dark cave, that memory.

His climb felt powered by the anger that he now let out through his hands and feet. It was easy—hand over hand, foot up and pull.

Minutes passed. He paused to catch his breath, hanging onto the side. Looking up, he guessed he was about halfway.

No point in looking down. He'd know when he was there.

They had taken his mother.

Who had?

There had to be someone who knew what actually happened.

He climbed again. Breathing hard, he paused.

Don't look down.

Back up again.

And then, suddenly, he was there. He stepped up onto the catwalk surrounding the bulbous metal holding tank. Standing, he gripped the railing.

Don't look down.

Out, then, out at the town of Marigold, where he'd lived his whole life.

He could run away, he realized. He'd need money, but he had saved some. And he could make more—he was handy. He was big. He could pass for fifteen.

Maybe even older, with a little careful make-up. One Halloween, his mother had made him up as an old man with her eyebrow pencil. She had one hand on his face to steady him, while the other—

Into the cave.

He began a slow, steady walk around the circumference of the water tank. The walkway wasn't wide. One hand on the railing, his fingers trailed along the green metal that held so much water.

Halfway around the circumference he came to a set of small rungs on the tank, leading up.

He could go higher. He froze with indecision.

Why climb more? He'd made it.

Because to come all this way and not...he'd always wonder what it would have been like. Up there. Who he would have been.

He gripped the narrow rungs leading up, and began to climb the side of the otherwise smooth tank. Behind him, the sun cleared a cloud. All at once, he was bathed in warmth.

And entirely obvious to anyone watching. Someone could see him, call the cops.

Good. At least then he'd have someone to ask about his mother—and father—who might actually have answers. There was no trouble for him to get into—his father didn't care about the fight, didn't care about anything.

He was breathing hard again—not entirely from the climb—rung after rung—so high. His head and shoulders topped the dome of the tank. He was trembling.

There, he'd done it. He could go back down now.

No, he told himself sternly. You haven't been on the top until you have actually been on the top.

He argued with himself. But he didn't know, and couldn't tell, what was sense and what was stupidity.

All the way, then.

The rungs went up top, over the cap of the tank, to the very center of the dome. The high point. There, a box, maybe a meter or other measurement device, was secured to the surface. Nicholas climbed it, stomach down, flattened to the cool metal dome like a lizard.

When he ran out of rungs, he slowly turned himself over to sit up on the smooth tank, gripping the last one in his hands.

He realized that he'd been holding his breath and let himself fully inhale, and look around.

To the west, the coastal mountain range, gray-blue edged with white. To the east, the town, laid out like a child's play set. To the south, the green of farms. Hints of distant towns. To the north, more mountains, fog-shrouded.

And his house. His father's house, anyway.

The sun was warming the metal just a little. He stroked it, wondering how many people had been up here, and if he were the youngest or not.

What sort of people climbed things like this? He didn't know anyone who did. Could he be the first?

His fingers, idly tracing a bolt in the metal, found something that moved. He picked up a stone, a flat inch of gray with a thin vein of white going through it. It would have been unremarkable on the ground, nothing more than a bit of gravel.

But up here it was special for how entirely out of place it was.

He examined it. How had it gotten here? Dragged up two sets of ladders in the tread of someone's boot? Too big for that. In the pocket of a jacket, fallen out? Or hitched a ride in a maintenance guy's toolkit? Who knew.

The dome was otherwise clean. No stones, no trash, nothing.

It was a small mystery that didn't matter. For some reason that lightened Nicholas's spirit a bit. He rolled the stone between his fingers, feeling the smooth and rough bits, the cool temperature. For a moment, he forgot about the pains that lived in the cave.

Maybe, he thought, gazing at the small crevasses and tiny ridges of the rock, his father was actually innocent.

And maybe, after the house sold, the two of them could leave Marigold and go somewhere else. Start over.

Somewhere the pain wasn't. Somewhere without any dark caves.

CHAPTER

FIFTEEN

As Sanne walked with Keyton out of the forest, she was pleased to see that Keyton was managing to keep the remaining red-black energy well-contained in zir field.

Whatever had happened for Keyton in the forest, it seemed to have left zir calmer, if pensive.

They walked together in silence, passing through the Rosewood neighborhood, by the Marigold city library, and past the Hazelnut Cafe. In front of the cafe were red newspaper boxes filled with the high school's journalism department's publication, the Marigold Pollinator.

They came to the intersection of Applewood and Sunflower. From there, Keyton would go toward Sunrise Hills, and Sanne toward the Gaffon house.

"Call me any time," Sanne said.

"You mean it?"

"I'll keep my phone on all night long, even. For you."

Keyton smiled. Briefly, but sincerely. "Thanks."

Sanne watched Keyton walk the street toward Sunrise Avenue, then turn toward zir house.

She put her hand in her left pocket where the ring was wrapped in silk, just to make sure it was there.

What, she wondered, should she say to Nicholas Gaffon?

When in doubt, go with simple.

I think I have your ring.

As Sanne made her way toward the Gaffon residence, she settled herself in mind and spirit, sending her awareness like roots into the earth below. She slowed herself, breathing in and out as if she were a tree, envisioning the transpiring air through each pore.

Overhead, it was as if her leaves rustled in the breeze, her roots finding stability deep below the sidewalk at every step.

As she arrived at the Gaffon house, a gray and white bungalow, she slowed further, strolling the walkway that divided a high, uncut lawn. A dark navy sedan was parked unevenly in the driveway, one front wheel on the grass.

She paused at the front stoop. There, an aura of sorrow and grief seeped out from the house, mixed with the hum of chaotic churn.

Overhead, something creaked. Sanne looked, saw nothing, but had the distinct sense of being watched.

Hello there, she sent warmly.

She felt a suspicious regard, a flash of misery, and it was gone.

Interesting.

Sanne's fingertips found the smooth selenite stone in her pocket. She whispered a healing spell into the air, and knocked on the door. Minutes passed. She knocked again.

Nothing.

With a sigh, Sanne put a reluctant finger to the doorbell button.

In the etheric world, the doorbell was a beleaguered servant with one simple job: to issue a loud notice when jabbed. Rarely appreciated, often resented, the doorbell became the holder of the energies of the household, an unarmed defender against the outside world.

Ringing a doorbell was like poking a loud, undersocialized parrot.

She pressed. A buzzer sounded.

Empty, the doorbell seemed to say. *Lost.*

Who? Sanne asked the doorbell. *Who is empty? Who is lost?*

But doorbells were not conversationalists, and really, nowhere near as smart as the average parrot.

The door opened. A tall man filled the doorway, bearing a resemblance to the boy Sanne had seen in the principal's waiting room. His misbuttoned plaid shirt hung loosely over stained jeans.

He gave her an annoyed expression. "What?"

"Hello," she said with what she hoped was warmth, salted with a business-like tone. "You must be Nicholas's father."

Matthew Gaffon gave a curt unwelcoming nod.

"I'm Susanne Pascral. I work with some of the kids who were part of the incident with Nicholas. At school."

Matthew Gaffon looked confused.

Sanne added: "The fight."

"The fight?" he asked.

"There was a fight between Nicholas and some other kids on Thursday," she said.

"Oh, that." Matthew Gaffon shrugged. "So?"

His tone was flat. More than flat—something was off.

In her pocket, Sanne touched the smooth tiger eye stone for clarity. She drew its perspective through herself and into the space between them, while solidifying the edges, creating a sort of bubble.

"Principal Hayes asked me," Sanne said, "if I might be able to talk with the kids involved. See if I could help everyone go forward without conflict." Not in those words. Close enough.

"First his attendance," Matthew Gaffon replied in a growling tone, "Then his grades. Now this. Leave him the hell alone."

"I was just wondering if I could talk to him for a few minutes."

"No," Matthew Gaffon said firmly. "Not a good time."

"I heard," Sanne said, sending a wave of care toward Matthew Gaffon, swirling it through the containing bubble. "I'm so sorry for your loss."

With that, Matthew Gaffon seemed to come fully and abruptly awake. He leaned forward toward her, as if about to lunge. "What did you hear? What makes you think you know anything at all about it?"

Sanne startled at his volume, caught herself, grounded into the earth, and deflected his anger to flow past her.

"I saw an announcement in the news. That's all," she said.

Thickening around Matthew Gaffon's torso, as if he were sweating it from his pores, was a pool of red-black. Bright and dark at the same time.

He was the source of the red-black. Now that she was here, faced with it, she saw just how powerful a wave it was.

Sanne took a step back, widening the bubble around them both to keep herself within. Her hand groped her pocket for another stone. Black tourmaline, this one, also called *schorl*. The crystalline ridges against her thumb were reassuring.

"I have something I think might be his," she said. As she spoke, Sanne thickened the air in the bubble, giving it substance and weight to slow down what was going on, because she didn't yet understand it. "Something he might have dropped. I'd like to return it to him if I can."

"Give it to me, and I'll give it to him."

The red-black energy around Matthew Gaffon was now so thick that it was as if he stood in a heavy cloud. It began to flow toward her.

Sanne quickly cast into the area between them a grayish-white puff, intended to dampen and absorb whatever it was that was coming toward her.

With her right hand she gripped the black tourmaline and tiger eye together, touching each other, and using them both, assembled a spell of balance and protection, subvocalizing. The spell took on the form of a flat square which she attached to the sides of the containing bubble, as if hanging out a glittering black sheet on a drying line between herself and Matthew Gaffon.

Or, more precisely, between Sanne and the red-black cloud drifting toward her. It concerned her, not knowing what it was, but in workings of this sort, it was essential to distinguish a person from the energies that they held. Or that held them.

The puff ball acted like cotton, absorbing some of the red-black miasma. Then red-black tendrils curled around it, consuming it.

Inside her left pocket, the ring was quiet. It might as well have been only a stone and metal. Was it afraid?

"I'd rather give it to him directly," Sanne said pleasantly, continuing the surface level conversation as she reinforced the glittering defensive shield so that it might withstand the pressure of the oncoming red-black wave.

Matthew Gaffon's face went blank. "You know what? I don't care. He's not here. Go away."

"Please, I only want to—" Sanne tried.

"Go away!" Matthew Gaffon barked. He turned, stepped into the house, and slammed the door.

Nearly all the red-black cloud went with him. Tendrils remained, but dissolved in Sanne's clearing spell.

Sanne stared at the closed door, trying to work out what had happened. After a few minutes, she let her defensive spell crumple and the bubble dissolve.

There was something wrong with Matthew Gaffon, that much was clear. He was generating a lot of power, in the form of the red-black he was emitting, whatever it was, but he did not seem to be controlling or directing it. It hadn't even really felt like an attack. More like a smoldering fire, with sticky fingers of smoke.

But whatever was causing the smoke was still burning. Sanne would bet that Matthew Gaffon didn't know about any of this. At least consciously.

Sanne turned and began to walk away, feeling unsettled. She had found the source of the red-black, but knew no more about what was causing it. Nicholas—the link between the fight and the father—might well shed light. If she could talk to him.

Sanne retraced her path homeward, feeling the warmth of the autumn sun. She passed the Hazelnut Cafe, paused, backed up, and went inside.

"Let me make a fresh pot," said Mike, the moment she walked in. With one hand, he brushed back his shaggy brown hair, and with the other, set the grinder going.

Sanne's fingers hovered over a bowl of candy corn on the counter.

"Better in memory," Mike warned with a grin.

Sanne laughed, took his advice to leave the candy corn undisturbed, and passed her phone over the register to pay.

Mike poured a cup, set it on the counter for her. Sanne inhaled the nutty scent, carrying the hot mug outside. There she sat and puzzled over the encounter with Matthew Gaffon.

Where, she wondered, was Nicholas Gaffon?

CHAPTER

SIXTEEN

It was a great view. It really was.

And Nicholas found that his thoughts did indeed feel they had more room to think.

Though in truth, he wasn't thinking much. Mostly he was sitting in the sun on the warming copper-green metal dome, and staring out at the horizon.

Up here, it almost felt as if the bad stuff in his life might not be able to find him.

At least for the moment. And for the moment, that would do.

Time went by. Eventually it occurred to him that he was going to need to pee. For a moment, he was tempted to stand and urinate over the side. But no, that was not how he was raised. You peed where you were supposed to. At least behind a tree.

So he would need to climb back down.

He wondered if it was going to be scary, descending, but it wasn't. He was already high, the risk taken. If he could go up, he could go down.

A few minutes later he stood on the ground, if not exactly happy, something like satisfied.

The greenspace around the tower had a few trees, some brush.

He found one, in an area mostly hidden from view, and emptied his bladder against its trunk.

As he did, he heard the top of the tree rustle in a way that didn't sound quite right, given the mild breeze.

Ignore it, he decided, zipping up. If he didn't give the weird sounds attention, maybe they'd go away.

Now what? He didn't want to go home. And given how his father had been lately, he doubted the man would even notice Nicholas was gone. Even if he did, he wouldn't be able to reach him on the mobile Nicholas had left in his room.

Nicholas was free to go anywhere.

He'd read a story about a guy who hopped rides on freight trains, seeing the whole country from the open door of a rail car.

Tempting.

The library, he decided. The Marigold public library, where he'd been to study. Chances were good no one would look for him there.

Who would look, anyway?

He'd walk the aisles of books, let his mind wander across worlds—the way it had found space across the open air on top of the water tower. A good plan.

He turned left on Ash, then right on Maple, heading toward Main, mind lost in thought, gaze on the sidewalk, and distracted enough that he almost walked into someone.

He stopped to mutter an apology and looked up.

It was her. The girl who had attacked him at school on Thursday. Keyton something.

He stepped back.

"What are you doing here?" she asked in an obnoxious tone.

"What are you," Nicholas retorted. "I live here."

"I do, too," she said belligerently.

Were they fighting? The conversation was already inane, and Nicholas shook his head, unsure. This was the last person he wanted, or expected, to run into. He felt unnerved, his fragile calm of the last hour shattered.

Her face was slender, brown hair cut short. She wore baggy pants, a backpack over her shoulders and wore a faded blue hoodie. Her hands were in her pants pockets. Both of them.

"What's it got in its nassty little pocketses?" Nicholas asked.

Why had he said that? Just asking for things to go badly. For her to get offended, and start another fight, right here on the street.

Then he'd be in more trouble, because he was nearly twice her size and everyone would assume he started it.

But no—she laughed.

"It must give us three guesseses, my precious!" she hissed.

His mouth fell open in surprise. He grinned in spite of himself.

Also, he realized he had his own hand in his own pocket, fiddling with the bit of gravel he'd taken from the top of the water tower. He pulled his hand out, empty, and held them both high.

Keyton mirrored him.

"Handses! Handses!" They both said together.

"A knife!" Nicholas said.

"String!" Keyton barked.

"Or nothing!" Nicholas finished.

They both laughed.

This was crazy—Nicholas felt that he had walked into an alternate universe, where enemies somehow already knew your favorite book.

Though, was she an enemy? They had fought, but Nicholas didn't really know what her deal was, only that she was aggressive and hit way harder than he'd expected from someone her size.

His expression sobered. So did hers.

"How do you know all that?" he asked her.

Keyton shrugged. "Practically my favorite movie."

"Movie!" Nicholas said, offended. "What about the book?"

"There's a book?" Keyton asked.

Nicholas gave a scoff and a groan. Why didn't people read

books? So stupid—the movies almost always lacked the really good stuff.

"Published in 1937," he said tightly. "Hell yeah, there's a book."

Keyton grinned. "Just messing with you. The book is way better."

Nicholas snorted, half-annoyed, half-amused. "Yeah, it is. I first read it when I was eight."

"Me, too," Keyton replied, sounding surprised.

She was, Nicholas reflected, actually a bit cute, in an elvish sort of way.

"And you know what?" Keyton said. "My teachers said it was too advanced for me. But at home, my mom told me to ignore them and..."

Nicholas had stopped breathing. Keyton's words stumbled to a halt. She looked down at the ground.

"Shit," Keyton said. "I'm sorry."

"Yeah? Not sorry you tripped me and kicked and punched me, but sorry my mother's dead?" The words just slipped out, and they were nasty.

His eyes watered, and he blinked, trying to clear them, expecting her to attack him again.

Maybe this time he wouldn't try to defend himself. Maybe she'd hit so hard that he'd black out. Maybe that wouldn't be so bad.

But Keyton did something else completely. She looked at him, tilted her head, and her expression shifted into something like sympathy and care.

He couldn't bear it. He looked away.

"You like books," he said after a moment.

"Yeah," Keyton replied.

"I was just going to the library," Nicholas found himself saying, wondering where his words were going. "Wanna come?"

Oh. That's where.

Keyton was silent for what seemed too long. *Never mind,*

Nicholas would say, which would sound lame. *If you're going that way, I mean.* Even lamer.

Suddenly he wanted to know what Keyton's favorite book was.

"Yeah, okay." Keyton said, turning to walk in the direction of the library. Nicholas skipped to catch up.

For a while they walked, saying nothing.

"So what do you have in your pocket?" Nicholas asked.

"You first."

"Tell you what," Nicholas said. "I'll trade you finding out what's in my pocket for you showing me a book you like at the library."

Keyton looked like she was almost going to smile.

"Only if you do the same," Keyton said.

"Deal."

CHAPTER

SEVENTEEN

Sanne sat at a metal table outside the Hazelnut Cafe, sipping from a white ceramic mug, and musing on the encounter with Matthew Gaffon.

Now what?

Laundry, probably. Her new house had a washer and dryer, which felt like the most amazing luxury.

Even so, she had put off washing clothes for what—two weeks now? And she had an upcoming wildcrafting class to schedule, emails to reply to asking for details that she had yet to decide. Little things like when, where, and how much.

The teens would come back to her place Monday and Tuesday. Maybe by Wednesday when they returned to school, one of them would be calm enough to talk to Nicholas and ask if he'd be willing to chat with Sanne about the ring.

Her phone cawed then trilled, which got her a disapproving look from a white-haired man in a pale lavender jogging suit two tables over, who was reading the Marigold Pollinator.

He should have heard what Sanne had on her phone before, when her ringtone had been the guttural bark of a Great Blue Heron. That had drawn some astonished looks from the people in Marigold, so she'd toned it down.

Sanne felt the caller then looked at the number.

It was the guy who claimed to be her brother. Who Marla had told her not to answer. *Text him. Tell him to talk to your lawyer. Give him my name and number.*

But to not answer...

You've got the heart and sense of a baby fawn, Sanne.

A youngling doe, at least, surely, Sanne thought wryly, staring at the phone in indecision.

She swiped up. "Hello," she said.

"Allen here again. I wanted to give you some time to think. Circling back. I know it might be a bit of a shock to find out that..."

Weakly, Sanne cut in. "My lawyer..."

A moment's silence. "Yes?" he prompted.

"She thought you might want to talk to her."

"Did she?" Allen sounded amused. "Sure, no problem. Want to text me her name and number?"

"That would be great," Sanne said, not feeling great. Or even good. She shifted uncomfortably in her seat. "Why are you so certain you're my brother? You never said."

Marla would approve of this line of questioning, surely.

After a moment's silence, he spoke. "Good question. Wish I could answer. But I think you just told me you're represented by a lawyer, and you want me to talk to them, not you. Did I get that right?"

Lawyer. And sister. Maybe his sister, too, now that she thought about it.

Her sister, who showed love for Sanne by getting legal on other people.

"Yes," Sanne said uncertainly.

"Got it. Because once you say that, I can only talk to your lawyer, not you. Rules, you know."

"Oh," Sanne said.

He must have caught her tone. "Just trying to be respectful."

Sanne felt the tug of his tone, imagining how he must feel. She clenched her jaw, clamping down on what she wanted to say.

They'll play on your kindness and care, Marla had warned. *Heart and sense of a baby fawn.*

"I'll talk to your lawyer," he said.

"Oh."

"Bye, then. Take care."

"Uh."

Allen had already hung up.

Sanne sat there, feeling all kinds of unsettled. It was hard to accept that people might come at her pretending to be friends, or family, to manipulate her for something as meaningless as money.

But it was quite easy to imagine what Marla would say to Sanne if she found out that Sanne talked to him.

Sanne exhaled heavily and texted Marla's name and number to her last caller, then set that number to go to voicemail.

She wasn't cut out for this, she decided, staring into her white mug and the last inch of cooling coffee. She stared across the street, into memory.

Did her parents have secrets that they had intended to tell Sanne and Marla when they were old enough to understand? Could one of those secrets have been a sibling?

Maybe an affair. Maybe he was a half-brother.

Sanne didn't like that thought. And she couldn't imagine her parents cheating on each other. They were just too good together.

Or so it had seemed when she was eleven.

She blinked, her subconscious tapping her on the shoulder. She had just seen two figures turn the corner, then walk out of sight. For a moment, she thought they'd looked like Keyton and Nicholas.

Talk about unlikely. A sweet thought from her subconscious, though, to imagine that rift repaired.

Perhaps the first step to making it so.

She stood and stretched, and went back into the cafe to return her white mug to the bus-bin.

Outside again, the sun had cleared another cloud. The warmth felt good.

"I heard there was a woman giving forest classes. That you?" asked the white haired man in the pale lavender jogging suit, scowling.

"I think so," Sanne said, still distracted by how she felt from the call with Allen. "I do lead wildcrafting outings."

"Made me think of it, that ringtone of yours. I used to be an active birder. That a towhee, is it?"

Sanne was surprised. The man had the same expression on his face now that he'd had before, the one she had taken as disapproval. And yet, here he was, expressing interest, his face still in a frown.

She looked at him again, beyond appearances, taking in his field of vibrancy and aliveness.

There I go again, Sanne thought irritably, *certain I can read other people's minds from their faces. I should just read their energy and ignore the words altogether.*

"Could I get a card?" he asked.

"I don't have any cards," Sanne admitted.

"Give you my number? You let me know when the next class is?"

"Sure." She handed him her phone. He typed in his name and number and handed it back.

"Thanks for..." she began, not quite sure how to finish. "For being interested."

He nodded, and Sanne realized that his face simply had a resting scowl. It didn't mean anything at all.

"Have a good," he said, and turned back to his newspaper.

"You, too."

Sanne strolled, enjoying the quiet afternoon of this small town. She put a hand in her right pocket to grip a smooth selenite stone, letting it settle her.

She turned onto Hidden Oaks, admiring a particularly

enthusiastic rosemary bush. A hummingbird darted from one purple bloom to another.

Returning the selenite nugget, she touched the tiger eye and black tourmaline, appreciating their help earlier, and wondered if Matthew Gaffon's red-black cloud was connected to his wife's death.

And where was Nicholas?

She slid a hand into her left pocket to check on the ring. Her fingertips found the white silk pocket square, soft and smooth.

But the ring wasn't there. The silk had nothing in it. Her pocket was empty.

Sanne sprinted back to the Hazelnut Cafe. She dropped down to hands and knees on the sidewalk to search under table and chair, running fingertips along the baseboard of the building seeking a gap large enough for a ring to roll into.

She dashed inside, described the ring.

Mike shook his dark, shaggy head. "Haven't seen it, sorry. Keep an eye out, though."

Desperation spurred her to search inside the cafe as well, popping up and down to scan the floor under tables. The cafe was empty but for a couple with a baby in a stroller, who she recognized from the weekly farmers market. Had they seen a ring? They hadn't.

Outside again, she sat on the curb at the street, looking up and down the gutter. How far could it have rolled?

She would have sworn it was secure in her pocket, wrapped in silk. But it was not there now.

When was the last time she knew for sure that she had it?

As she had approached the Gaffon residence, wondering what to say to Nicholas, she had put her hand in her pocket, feeling metal and stone through silk.

She checked again—no holes in this pocket. She'd reinforced it herself. It only took you one time losing something valuable through a pocket hole to become meticulous about such things.

It couldn't have fallen out. But it had.

Her imagination reminded her of the overgrown grass outside the Gaffon house. Mind spinning, she ran three blocks toward the Gaffon residence, then stopped abruptly, breath coming hard.

She had to think this through.

Could Matthew Gaffon have somehow taken it from her?

No, he'd come nowhere near her.

By sorcery, then?

Such power was rare. Beyond rare. If Matthew Gaffon were that kind of energy worker, Sanne would have noticed it the moment she met him. He wasn't right, with that red-black smoke around him like an illness, but he wasn't that.

Sanne strode forward again, feeling urgency to act, then shuffled to a stop. Her heart rate was up, but she had to admit that her sense was down. In a heightened state of stress it was easy to miss things.

Okay, then. What did she know for sure?

The ring was gone, where and how were in the realm of mystery, where she must for the moment allow them to stay.

She took a lengthy breath, exhaling it with meticulous slow control. And did it again. She cast a calming spell on herself.

A minute of that, and Sanne could feel her body shift from agitated readiness into something a little quieter.

Don't look only at what you can see, her mother used to say. Her mother, her first teacher.

Sanne took the selenite stone in her left hand, the tiger eye in her right, seeking balance, feeling for a door to the unseen.

She turned in place. *Move slower.* She felt the soles of her boots brush the sidewalk, her vision softening to take in what was around her.

The scent of decaying Autumn leaves. Someone baking—pie,

if she wasn't mistaken. Lavender flowers from a nearby bush. The hint of damp dog.

Across the street, a two-story green Craftsman was surrounded by flowering lavender and wine-colored smoke trees.

Even slower.

At her side, a grassy yard was dotted with brightly colored children's toys. From a Japanese maple hung a swing.

Another turn of the arc.

A large, blond dog lay on the raised porch of a white, single story house, watching her.

No, not watching her. Watching something else, beyond her.

Sanne turned her head. Diagonally from where she stood was the white-haired man she'd spoken with at the cafe, about to stride around the corner. Had she not looked at just that moment, she would have missed him entirely.

"Hello," Sanne called out, realizing that she didn't know his name.

"There you are," he said, arms up for a moment in exasperation. He changed direction to come her way. Frowning he said, "Thought you might have called me by now."

"I promise I'll text you about my next class when I get home," Sanne replied.

He shook his head and held up his other hand. "Your ring. You dropped it."

Sanne's mouth fell open. "You have my ring?"

He looked both ways as he crossed the street toward her. "I'd say, rather, it has me. I don't think it likes me much, but it won't let me go. Reminds me of my ex-wife."

"What?" Sanne asked, bemused.

He held up his right hand. There, on his smallest finger, was the ring.

"Oh," Sanne breathed, overcome with relief.

He pulled on his finger. "See? Won't come off. After you left, I saw something shiny on the ground. Picked it up. Slip off your finger?"

"It was in my pocket," Sanne said.

"Try your finger next time. Figured the safest way not to lose it while looking for you was for me to wear it. Been criss-crossing the neighborhood ever since, trying to find you, since you have my number, but I don't have yours. Got my exercise for the day, anyway." He looked like he was trying to smile, but the effort only changed the shape of his scowl.

"What makes you think it doesn't like you?" Sanne asked, her gaze on the ring.

He held up his hand. The six-pointed star in the night-sky-blue sapphire was dim now. Barely a dot.

He made a thoughtful sound. "Do things ever talk to you?"

All the time.

"Depends on what you mean by talk," Sanne replied cautiously.

He tilted his head a bit, as if to concede the point. "Old birder here. I used to try to suss out what the birds were saying with their calls and songs. Figured it had to be a bit more nuanced than 'hey!' or 'my branch' or 'you're cute'. I got kind of used to listening that way. Probably my imagination, but now I sometimes think I hear things talk. Sure it sounds crazy to you."

"Not at all. Go on."

"So I put this on, and then it gets all huffy and keeps saying it needs you. Mind you, I don't even know your name, but I could feel it calling—you. Now it won't let me go."

"Let me try?" Sanne asked.

He held out his hand. Sanne put fingers on the band of silvery white gold, and gently tugged.

It slipped off.

"Good riddance, you little beast," the man said to the ring. Sanne closed her fingers around it, gripping it tightly.

It was the first time she had touched it with her own skin. It felt...grateful?

"Thank you so much," Sanne said. "Uh..."

"Tom Howe." He held out a hand.

"Susanne Pascral," she said, taking his hand with hers, still gripping the ring tightly in the other.

Later, if he did join her class, there'd be a chance to give him her friend-name. Not to mention probably not charging him at all for the class, given how grateful she was.

"See you around, Susanne. Maybe wear it. Have a good," he said, waving as he strolled away, and around the corner.

Sanne opened her hand to examine the ring. It seemed content, like a tiny purring cat, curling on the pillow of her hand in the sun.

Hello, ring, Sanne sent. *Do you want to travel on my finger?*

She felt the ring shift, from ease to tension.

Nicholas, it said.

A glimmer of understanding caught up with Sanne, offering a theory.

It was no accident that the ring came out of her pocket as she was sitting there drinking coffee, any more than it had been an accident it came out of Nicholas's pocket in the Principal's waiting room.

The ring was searching.

Nicholas, it said again, with more urgency.

And the ring would keep escaping pockets until it found what it sought. Whatever or whoever that was.

So if Sanne put this ring on her finger, and it didn't come off, she was in this whole situation—the ring's quest—until it was resolved. And who knew how long that might be?

It seemed quite clear to her that it was unwise to don an enchanted ring without understanding what it was capable of, or where the quest might lead.

But also quite clear was that it was even more unwise to put it into her pocket again, and assume it would stay.

She looked at the dog, who gazed back at her. She imagined it watching all this and thinking: *Glad I'm a dog.*

She snorted, looked up at the sky, then the ground, and brushed the tiger eye stone in her pocket, asking for guidance.

Stone or sense led her to what now seemed obvious: She was already in it. Might as well go all the way.

She put the ring on her ring finger. It fit, and snugly.

When she tried to take it off again, she was unsurprised to find it stuck.

EIGHTEEN

Keyton and Nicholas sat outside the library on the wide edge of a cement planter box in which various colorful flowers grew. One of them was purple and spiky and looked to Keyton like it belonged in a salad.

Inside the library, the two of them had shown each other books they liked and recommended, had checked out a few, and had come outside to do the second part of the deal: find out what was in their pockets.

They both had rocks.

"Yours is nicer," Nicholas said, holding out his irregular dark gray nugget, a white streak going through it.

"You got yours from the top of the water tower," Keyton said. "I got mine from a box." And then, when that didn't seem like enough, "I like yours."

They sat facing a wide walkway that led from the library to the parking lot. On either side, mown green lawn stretched wide enough that some older kids tossed a red Frisbee back and forth. The day was warm. The breeze was sweet.

Things didn't seem so bad.

Keyton once again reflected on the strangeness of this

moment. On the one hand, this guy sitting next to zir was the ass who had called Keyton names.

On the other hand, he liked books, knew some of them as well as Keyton did—which had never happened before—and had made Keyton laugh a whole lot in the last hour or two. He was funny, in a good way.

And laughter? There hadn't been much of that lately.

Also, he'd climbed the water tower. Which was cool.

"I climbed a utility pole a few weeks ago," Keyton said, wondering if that would sound like a pathetic comparison.

"No way," Nicholas said, sounding impressed.

"Yeah," Keyton replied, reassured. "Not as high. But..." But what? "But high."

"But how did you do that? There's nothing to grab onto."

"Easy," Keyton said. "I had equipment. A belt. Climbers that strap to your leg and ankle, so you have a spur every step." Keyton gestured at zir pink and green court shoes, which, now that Keyton thought about it, were the same color as the watermelon tourmaline with which ze was gesturing. "Though, next time, I'll think I'll wear gloves."

"Yeah, me too," said Nicholas, looking at his palm, which was a bit red.

"You were higher," Keyton said.

"You were climbing a pole."

"And it was five in the morning. Dark." Now Keyton was definitely bragging, but so what.

"Woah. I had full daylight."

Keyton liked Nicholas's voice. "You were higher."

Nicholas laughed. "You said that already."

Was that a mocking laugh? Keyton turned to look at him. It didn't seem to be.

"You hit me kind of hard," Nicholas added while Keyton was looking at him.

"Oh, man." Keyton looked down, feeling abruptly unsettled. Turning the tourmaline stone between fingers, Keyton said: "I know I did. I'm..." *Sorry.* The word just wouldn't come. "I probably shouldn't have."

"I guess I also said some stuff," Nicholas said.

"You sure did," Keyton said, trying to sound annoyed, or hurt, or offended, but not quite able to summon the feeling. Just two days ago, but it seemed like years back.

"Your gender thing. I don't get you," Nicholas said.

"Yeah, that's expected," Keyton shot back, snatching the backpack from the flower bed and standing.

"What?" Nicholas asked. "What are you doing?"

Now Keyton felt the anger. "Going."

"Oh, fine way to make friends," Nicholas said sarcastically.

Friends? At that, Keyton paused, gripping the watermelon tourmaline tightly.

The anger management class came back, as did Sanne's words.

Okay, worth a try. *Breathe. Do it again. Super slow.*

Huh, it worked.

Now Keyton also remembered about the red-black sticky stuff, how Sanne had cleaned the stone and managed to keep it clean. That red-black was probably all over Nicholas right now, if Keyton could only see it.

"Yeah, well, I'm not very good at that either," Keyton muttered, returning the backpack to the plants, and sitting down again next to Nicholas. After a moment: "You called me little miss weirdo."

"Huh," Nicholas said, "Well, you are little, compared to me. And weird. In a good way, I think. You don't feel like a girl?"

"Shit, I have to explain myself?"

"No," Nicholas said. "I'm just asking."

Keyton gripped the watermelon tourmaline. It still felt clear of the red-black stuff. Somehow.

Weird that Keyton could tell.

Keyton looked over at Nicholas, trying to suss out if he was truly interested, or just looking for an opening to say something mean again, the way Keyton's parents were always doing with each other.

Nicholas looked back. He didn't say anything. Somehow Keyton found that more convincing than any words he could have used.

"Sometimes I feel like a girl," Keyton said quietly. "Sometimes I feel like a boy. Other times like neither. Or both at once."

Nicholas made a thoughtful sound. He toyed with his small rock.

"My mother died," he said.

"Oh, man. I'm sorry," Keyton blurted out, and meant it. Somehow that had been lost in the conversation. What to say next, Keyton had no idea.

Sanne would know.

Keyton gave in to impulse. "You want to see my stone?" and offered the watermelon tourmaline out to Nicholas.

Sure, he'd get the red-black stuff all over it again, but Sanne could clean it later. Or maybe Keyton could learn how.

"Yeah," Nicholas replied. "You want to see mine?"

"Yeah."

They traded stones and sat there for a while, each of them examining the other's rock.

"Do you believe in ghosts?" Nicholas asked.

"No," Keyton replied promptly, then thought over the last year with Sanne, Rufus, and Angie, learning to knit, learning to make spells. Fighting a baby demon. Using magic stones. "Maybe," Keyton amended.

"I think I have one. I think it's my Grandma Trinity. I think she's really unhappy. I'm afraid I might know why."

"Why?" Keyton prompted breathlessly.

"I think my father did something to my mom. I don't know. I don't know if I want to know. And I don't know what to do."

The depth of pain in Nicholas's voice tore at Keyton insides. If only Sanne were here now. She would know what to do.

"I know someone who might be able to help," Keyton said.

"Yeah?"

Keyton nodded. "Do you want me to ask?"

"Yeah," Nicholas said.

A maroon SUV pulled up to the curb. Five ten-year olds piled out, squealing and laughing, skipping and running their way to the library. A woman got out to follow. She smiled and waved at the driver, who waved back, and drove off, presumably to park.

Keyton saw the affection in that smile and wave. So obvious that those two adults really liked each other.

The group of kids made their noisy, happy way past the planters and into the library.

Keyton remembered being that age, remembered what it was like to have parents who cared about each other, who weren't always yelling about divorcing.

The sun had gone behind a cloud.

No, it had gone behind the building.

"Hey, what time is it?" Keyton asked.

Nicholas shrugged.

Keyton pulled the backpack closer, and fished out zir phone. Numerous missed calls, from both parents. The usual.

"Oh, man, it's nearly three. I gotta go," Keyton said, bemused at how late it had gotten.

"Me, too, I guess," Nicholas replied.

Keyton looked at Nicholas, then did a double take. For a split second, Keyton could actually see the red-black stuff all over Nicholas, could see lines of it flicker and swirl around the tourmaline rock in his palm.

Then it was gone, and it was Nicholas sitting there.

Wow.

"What?" Nicholas asked. "You want your stone back?"

"No, you hold onto it for now."

"Okay."

"You want yours?"

"Naw, you keep it. For now."

Keyton had always found goodbyes to be such a pain,

especially when you were confused about how you felt, and weren't sure if you were seeing that red-black stuff or just imagining it. Keyton grabbed the backpack, then waved over zir shoulder while calling "bye" and wondering if Nicholas was watching or not, and if he was, what he was thinking.

Halfway home, Keyton realized that the two of them hadn't exchanged any contact information. And Keyton had entirely forgotten to mention the ring.

Keyton stopped on the sidewalk and texted Sanne.

Hey I have someone who maybe has a ghost. can u help?

CHAPTER
NINETEEN

Sanne returned home, began laundry, made herself some food, and finally checked her phone.

Happy to try, Sanne texted back to Keyton. *Who?*

He thinks maybe his grandma Trinity.

Sanne blinked for a moment in confusion.

Teenagers, she reflected, were utterly fascinating. They knew so much about life, could dive into the most exacting details, and yet still miss the glaringly obvious.

Of course, that described many adults, too.

I mean, Sanne typed, *who is the someone who maybe has a ghost?*

Nicholas G.

Then it hadn't been her imagination, sitting at the cafe, thinking she saw Keyton and Nicholas walking together. She had.

That's what you got for not actually seeing what you were looking at, she thought wryly.

Could this ghost be the spirit Sanne had felt at the house?

If the ring was connected to Nicholas's mother Gail, and the ghost was the grandmother, were they at odds with each other? Working together?

Or confused, and caught between worlds, as ghosts so often were.

How did the red-black smoke figure in? What was Matthew Gaffon's role in all this?

I'd like to talk to him, she texted Keyton.

I have to get my rock back.

Sanne frowned at this seeming non sequitur.

Does he know I have his ring?

No.

Can you tell him, and text me his number? Or give him mine?

Didn't get. Maybe go to his place tomorrow. Arg parents GTG.

And with that, the conversation was over.

Sanne slid open the glass doors to the backyard and stepped out to watch the fading light, the sky red and yellow and indigo against a distant treeline.

From the exchange with Keyton, she knew a few things she hadn't before. First, that Keyton and Nicholas had met, talked, and somehow traded rocks rather than blows. A good sign.

Next, that Keyton was planning to see Nicholas again, possibly tomorrow. *Maybe.*

Well, maybe would have to be good enough for now.

Sanne let out a long stream of air as she examined her hand in the dimming light. The ring's white star pulsed slightly.

And lastly, that there was a ghost, and it might be Nicholas's grandmother, named Trinity.

There wasn't much she could do tonight. She could hardly go back and case the Gaffon house at night, looking for a maybe-ghost. Especially given the interaction with Matthew Gaffon.

For now at least Keyton would have a better chance at furthering the quest, whatever it was.

Nicholas, the ring whined.

"You'll have to make do with me for now," Sanne told it. "Maybe tonight I sing you a song instead?"

The service was over, and while it had been a good one, something about compassion, this was the part Rufus liked best: food.

Rufus heaped Morton Hutherson's bean salad onto his plate, then one of Lee Collins's hotdogs—okay, he'd take two—and a mountain of chips. He grabbed a cup of water and went to sit at the wood picnic table under the old pine tree.

Pinecones crunched satisfyingly underfoot, rolling a little under his shoes and smelling awesome.

Rufus set his plate of food on the table, took a swig of the water, and wondered what Angie was doing. Did her family attend one of the other churches in Marigold? Somehow he suspected not.

So he imagined her at home, eating pancakes and bacon and laughing with her parents. Maybe her brother was back visiting from college. Probably they'd all go out to a park. Play ball. Frisbee.

Or maybe she was doing homework. No, she'd have caught up already.

He looked around the yard, full of adults and kids. Adults gathered by the food table talking. The smaller kids were chasing each other around at the mini-playground, off to the side toward the fenceline, swinging on swings, climbing up a blue plastic slide.

Rufus wondered if Angie would like his folks, his congregation.

"Hi, Rufus."

Rufus glanced to his side. A pale print dress with daisies and pink flowers. A gold chain around a thin, pale wrist.

"Hey, Diane," he said.

Dozens of people milled around in the yard. There were, he now realized as he took a good look, no other Black families here. Would Angie feel out of place? She never did with him and Keyton, so probably she'd be good.

"How's it going?" Diane asked.

"Fine," Rufus replied, taking another swig of water. He looked up through spiky branches of pine. It was a little tree, he realized, at least compared to Sanne's three huge ancient trees in the forest. By their standard, a baby, probably. Or a teenager, anyway.

But before Sanne, Rufus used to think of this pine as a big tree, because you could hide behind its trunk if you were careful. When he was smaller, he used to do that, playing with other kids after the sermon.

"I don't go to your school," Diane said. "So I only see you here."

"That's true," Rufus said, nodding slowly.

Over by the potato salad stood his mother, his father was whispering in her ear. Probably reassuring her that the salad was good, even if she'd taken Rufus's advice and added toasted coconut flakes. And no, he might be saying, it didn't have too much pepper.

Or maybe something more personal than that. Just then his father laughed a little and his mother smiled, a really big smile, and Rufus remembered that the kid in the fight, Nicholas, had just lost his mother.

The thought sent a chill of pain through Rufus's middle as he imagined losing his own. It would suck so much.

"Hey, dimwit."

Rufus turned. William sat where Diane had been a moment ago.

"What?" Rufus asked. How had she come and gone so fast with him hardly noticing?

"The prettiest girl at church, and you give her the cold. What TF anyway?"

"Hey," Rufus said sharply at this almost-swearing. He stole a glance at the pastor, who fortunately was well out of earshot, over by the desserts. "What are you talking about?"

William, like Diane, went to Lupine Middle School. William tied back his shoulder-length, caramel colored hair at church, to keep it orderly. But he wore sunglasses now, which Rufus assumed was so no one would forget how cool he was.

"I'm saying she likes you," William said.

"She does not."

William sighed. It was one of those sighs that said William thought Rufus was an idiot.

"She's hung up on you," William said. "You can't even see it. Hence the 'dimwit' of my opening. Look, if you don't like her, tell her you have a girlfriend or something so the rest of us have a chance at her epic-ness. What don't you like about her, anyway?"

"Never thought about it. I guess her hair is sort of blonde."

"Sort of? You don't like blondes?" William asked, in a tone that said that was the stupidest thing he'd heard in a long time.

Rufus thought about his own hair, which was red, or rather, a sort of dark rust. Somehow blonde seemed wrong.

"Yeah, I don't."

"Your loss, loser," William said, but not meanly. He gave Rufus a friendly pat on the shoulder. "Just kick her loose, eh?"

"That's not my—" But William had already pranced off to the food table. "Thing," Rufus finished, feeling entirely lost in this whole sudden drama.

The good thing about church was that even though Rufus had grown up around most of these kids, he only saw them once a week. By the time next Sunday came around, a lot of things would be forgotten. Maybe even forgiven.

Or maybe, Rufus reflected, he really was just clueless.

He shrugged and went around to the other side of the tree, out of sight. He sat on a layer of pine needles and grass at the base and pulled out his phone to play Minecraft.

Instead, he brought up Angie's contact and opened up text. "Happy Sunday!" he typed, then backspaced over it. "How's it going?" which he also erased.

Never mind. It didn't matter—he'd see her tomorrow. They were going back to Sanne's to do stuff, maybe with yarn, or magical stuff, and then the forest, which was always good.

Maybe Rufus would invite Angie to Sunday worship sometime. He'd have to figure out just how to pitch it, the way he'd pitched Marigold Middle School instead of homeschooling to his dad.

Sanne had helped with that. He could maybe ask Sanne about this pitch, too. Or maybe he'd figure it out himself.

Or maybe—and the thought came softly, as if it were not quite sure of its footing—he'd invite her somewhere just the two of them.

As fast as the thought came, it left. Rufus was dimly aware that he'd helped it exit the stage of his mind, because it was a thought he didn't quite know what to do with.

He sighed, closed the message app, and brought up Minecraft.

At least this game he knew how to play.

CHAPTER

TWENTY

"I wanted to return your rocks," Angie said. "Thank you very much."

Sanne, in robe and flannel pajamas, and again awoken from a dead sleep, stared at Angie just outside her door.

She stood in the same spot Keyton had the prior morning, and—Sanne glanced at the clock to be sure—at just about the same time.

"We didn't schedule this, did we," Sanne said, with a sense of déjà vu.

"No. I'm sorry if I woke you," said Angie. Very polite.

Too polite. Though Sanne was struggling to focus, she could tell that Angie was standing stiffly, her energy tight.

"Come in," Sanne said. "Let me make myself coffee." She yawned into her hand, and turned to pad into the kitchen, not watching to see if Angie was following. "Get you something?" she called over her shoulder.

"No, that's all right. But I don't need to...I didn't mean to..."

Sanne was betting that Angie hadn't planned to come in at all. She puttered with the hot water kettle and ground some coffee, setting up cone and filter, and listening for Angie's next move.

At last, she heard the front door close and Angie's footfalls in the house.

Sanne's wager was that Angie would come in anyway, if Sanne acted as if it were expected. A wager won.

Sanne watched the coffee drip for the minute it took to fill the cup, giving Angie a moment to settle, then took her glass mug of hot brew to where Angie stood at the kitchen table.

Sanne sat, smiled. "Have a seat."

Angie set her stones on the table, then took a chair across from Sanne, her motions a mix of uncertainty and tension.

"What's up, Angie?" Sanne asked.

Angie took a deep breath. "It's great to work with you, Sanne. But I think maybe..." she looked away, clearly struggling.

"Did something happen?" Sanne asked.

"Nothing happened." Angie's tone was emphatic. "It's just that I already know a lot of the computer material you're teaching us. I don't mind going over it again, but I think maybe I need more advanced material than you provide."

Sanne felt parts of herself knot up, took a breath. "I'm happy to give you more advanced work," Sanne said. "I aim for whatever the group as a whole can—"

"That's just it," Angie said, tapping one of the stones on the table for emphasis, the black obsidian orb. "I think I've outgrown the group."

Sanne sat back, reassessing this shift. She said, "The last few days have been hard. Emotional whirls and energetic churn. Everyone needs a little space to digest. Give it time."

Angie looked like she wanted to snap back at that, which was unlike her. Her eyes were wide, her glare hard. Angie sat very still, staring at the black and purple stones on the table.

Sanne ached, trying not to let it show. She didn't want Angie to leave.

They weren't her kids, she told herself again.

And, Sanne reminded herself, she was supposed to be the

adult in the room, which meant getting a grip on her own emotions, and not letting them drive the bus.

"I'm guessing," Sanne said, "that you're upset at something that happened in the fight with the others, something that hasn't been talked about yet, and doesn't seem to be on the road to repair."

Angie's expression was taut. She gave a twitch of a shrug, followed by the tiniest of nods.

"I wonder if," Sanne continued, "the friendship you've had with Keyton and Rufus doesn't feel like much of a friendship right now."

Another barely perceptible nod.

Sanne nodded, too. "I think I missed a step. When the three of you were here the other day, after the classes, I didn't make a way for you to talk together about what happened at the fight. I thought you all needed time. Maybe I was wrong."

"You can't fix everything, Sanne."

The words had weight. As true as they were, Sanne knew how far she had gone and how far she would yet go to fix things for these kids.

"Anyway," Angie said, glancing at the kitchen and living room. "You have an inheritance now. You don't need the money. You won't miss me."

The words cut deep. Sanne took a ragged breath.

"Angie," Sanne said, unable to keep the pain from her voice. "It hasn't been about the money, not since the start. It's about you. The others, too, yes. But very much you. You're so fast. You remind me of...me."

Angie blinked slowly, her face still immobile.

A difficult trick, that one, Sanne knew, to keep your face a mask when you hurt so much. It was a skill learned only through rocky times.

"I won't hold you if you want to leave," Sanne said gently. "But..." She swallowed, struggling to get the words right. Were there any right words for this?

No. Only an ache demanding to be voiced.

Sanne's gaze met Angie's. Sanne felt an opening.

"Please wait," Sanne said, her tone unsteady. "At least until you three return to school. This suspension is a strange place and time. Things might change. Maybe enough that you remember why you called them friends."

"You, too, Sanne. I call you friend."

Angie's face was still an impassive mask, but a tear made its way from the corner of one brown eye down her dark cheek to fall onto the wooden table.

A gift. Sanne caught her breath, felt the gravity and courage in Angie's words.

Sanne whispered, "Would you let me make a healing spell for us both? Put the amethyst there, where your tear landed?"

Angie's expression softened, just a little. Enough. She slid the pale lavender-colored stone onto the damp wood, and gave a short exhale, like an aborted sob.

Sanne felt Angie's hurt, a twin to her own. She followed the sorrow in herself to the root: her mother and father's sudden death.

It wasn't enough to look through the window. You had to go through the door.

From that root she walked alongside grief to a deeper past yet. She shut her eyes, inviting her forebears to join her, sensing the struggle of generations, woven through with love and loss, like a weave of brightly colored yarn that brought with it the great wisdom of how to hold life's intensities.

"I have invited my ancestors to join us," Sanne said quietly. "You are welcome to do the same."

From Angie's surprised expression, Sanne guessed she had never considered this. Then, from the inward look, that she was willing to try.

In moments, Sanne felt a gathering presence of Angie's ancestors as well.

Welcome, she sent warmly.

Dim images mixed. The labor of decades, in cities, and farms. Trans-oceanic journeys, some free, some not. The stench of sewers, the perfume of orchards. Babies born, beloveds dying. Again and again the hands that gripped each other firmly, that now reached out to Sanne and Angie in the faith that this challenge, too, could be met.

Thus fortified by the spirits whose love and labor brought them both life, Sanne returned to the present, to this moment's grief. With tenderness, she wrapped it into a bundle as kindling for the spell to come.

The most sacred of magics must be approached this way: you cleaned up what you could while gently collecting the other quite messy parts. One could not make a spell out of a clean space alone, nor could one make it only from the chaotic detritus of human suffering. One must include both.

With the tinder of messy emotion, Sanne exhaled a flame of clarity—her own love, unencumbered by need—into the amethyst. She spoke her father's spell softly.

> Look to see
> Listen to hear
> Come with me
> Near and dear

The amethyst inhaled the spell. The pale lavender stone became imbued with an ethereal purple luminescence, as if it had just been hit by a ray of sunlight.

"Oh," Angie breathed.

The spell emanated from the stone, taking shape through their two sets of hands on the table, then rippling out to engulf them whole, like an ocean wave crashing in all directions.

"Oh, Sanne," Angie said. "I felt that."

Of course she did. Angie was on track to be as much a sorcerer as Sanne was, if she wanted to be.

They bathed in the healing wash of the spell, letting it work their edges and then into and through the torn, aching parts inside them both.

For Sanne, it touched places still tender from that darkest time in her life, the loss, and then after, when her uncle Jerry took Sanne and her sister Marla into his house. Her uncle, who had never had children, and didn't approve of his sister's strange practice, had no intention of letting eleven-year-old Sanne continue the foolishness.

The pain of losing her parents, then parts of herself, had been one tsunami after another. Sanne had changed. She had no choice.

Images came. The fire pit where her books burned. Her own screams as Jerry held her in the vise of his grip, forbidding her to rescue the burning notebooks. And then, across years, seeing how Jerry himself burned with a power he would never credit.

She remembered her resolve to never be that powerless again.

Then the letter, this spring. Jerry's final words did not, could not, change the past, but the apology gave Sanne a chance to begin again. To see the present differently.

You could be a healer, and still not be able to heal yourself.

Angie's expression had gone from guarded to open. She was glowing, like the amethyst itself. As Sanne watched, Angie took the spell inside. With the wordless encouragement of her own ancestors, began to work to make it her own.

Sanne watched in joy, pride, and amazement.

When at last the spell began to dissipate, Sanne reached for her coffee, her hands trembling slightly. She swallowed it down, a tonic and a healing.

You could tell when a spell had run its course, had done what it could do, because you started to come back to the present.

Sanne went to the sink and brought back a large glass of water for Angie, who drank it down, shaking her head when Sanne offered more.

Nothing pragmatic had been solved here, of course. There

must still be talk between Angie, Keyton, and Rufus, about what had happened and how to understand each other.

But the rips and tears of the spirit were never solved only by the pragmatic, which was best sorted out after the spirit had space to mend.

Angie took the amethyst stone in her hand. "I had no idea stones could do all that," she said.

"They didn't," Sanne replied. "I did. You did. The stone only helps hold and focus the work."

"Me?" Angie asked.

Sanne nodded. "A lot you, actually."

Angie smiled, then Sanne did, too.

CHAPTER

TWENTY-ONE

Sanne woke Monday morning early.

She looked at the clock. Seven am. She lay there, half-awake, waiting for the doorbell, which did not ring.

At last she gave up, got up, and padded to the kitchen.

Yesterday she had texted the kids, telling them to come anytime between nine and ten, not only to give Sanne a chance to sleep late—which she had not, of course—but to see how they arranged themselves and get information about their now-constellation.

Rufus arrived first, diving into conversation without preamble.

"Would you ever want to come to my church?" he asked earnestly. "After the sermon there's lunch. Mr. Hutherson makes a killer bean salad. My mother's potato salad is even better. But that's because she finally added capers, as I said she should, but a hard no to the wasabi. Anyway. Are you even allowed to?"

Sanne sat on the couch, and snorted, amused, coffee in hand. Rufus waited for an answer, bouncing back and forth with his extra energy.

Oh, to be fourteen again.

But no. Not worth it.

"I'm allowed, Rufus," she replied. "Just as you're allowed in the forest."

"What? Oh, I see. No, wait, I don't. Are you saying...What are you saying?"

"I'm saying that sacred spaces aren't limited to big houses with crosses on their roofs."

He stopped bouncing for a moment to consider. "Sure, okay." Then: "So what are we doing today?"

"Depends on all of you. What you want."

"Maybe we can get the weather station feed working," he said.

"Is that what Keyton put up on top of a utility pole?"

Rufus pushed out his lower jaw, the way he did when he was struggling with a problem.

"Are you not supposed to tell me?" Sanne asked.

"Not sure." He considered, then shrugged. "We got a used weather rig. Wanted to hook it up with the NOAA citizen weather thing, and have that be our school science project. But we couldn't get the data packet send working."

"And what about the pole?"

"Keyton's idea. Though, to be fair, I would have done it, if ze hadn't."

Angie was next to arrive, at precisely nine-thirty am, which somehow didn't surprise Sanne.

Now that she was paying closer attention to Angie, Sanne noticed she didn't look at Rufus. Not once.

But Rufus was looking at her. And in that looking, Sanne saw his energy reach out, an unaware question with a hint of vulnerability.

Sanne felt foolish for not having seen it before.

Well, maybe Rufus's attention was new. Maybe Angie knew about it and didn't like it. Maybe that's why she wanted out of the group.

Keyton was last to arrive, a bit after ten. But not alone.

"Hope it's okay," Keyton said, brushing past Sanne at the

door, in a tone that translated into: I know I should have asked, but I didn't think you'd say yes if I did.

Nicholas hesitantly followed Keyton into the house. He looked around the open space, up at the skylights, warily at Rufus, with a quick glance at Angie. His gaze came to rest on Sanne. The streak of red-black wound and snaked around him.

"You're the governess," Nicholas said.

Rufus barked a laugh, Keyton smiled, and Angie looked annoyed.

"Actually, I'm the computer science tutor," Sanne said.

Rufus glanced at Angie to see her reaction, then frowned. "She's other things, too," he said to Nicholas, and he took a step to put himself between Angie and Nicholas. "But you're not one of us."

"Hello, Nicholas," Sanne said, stepping into the center of the space described by the four teens, and slightly blocking Rufus. "It's nice to meet you. I think I have your ring."

That got Nicholas's full attention. "Where is it?"

Sanne held up her left hand, reversed, to show the side with the dark blue star sapphire stone.

"Can I have it back?"

"Of course. Well, maybe," Sanne said.

"What do you mean, maybe? It's mine."

Sanne tugged at the ring. "It doesn't come off."

She stepped closer to the mystified Nicholas, then tried again. Nope.

"Soap and water?" asked Angie.

"Don't think that'll do it," Sanne said. "Nicholas, would you try?" She held her hand out, fingers spread.

Nicholas tugged on the ring. "Stuck."

"You said you wanted Nicholas," Sanne said to the ring. "Here he is."

Matthew, the ring said.

Sanne's surprised expression must have caught their attention.

"What did it say?" Angie asked her.

"It talks?" asked Nicholas. His mouth grinned in amused skepticism.

"It's confused," Sanne said. "Or I am."

"What do you mean?" asked Keyton.

The time had come, Sanne judged, to get a few things out in the open. "Nicholas, what was your hope, coming here today?"

"Well," Nicholas said slowly. "Keyton said she—ze—might know someone who could..." He gave Rufus and Angie wary looks.

"It's okay," Keyton said of the other two. "They're my friends. You can tell them."

Nicholas gave a slow shrug, a seemingly reluctant acceptance, and looked down, not meeting anyone's gaze. "I think my grandmother's ghost—my mother's mother—wants to avenge my mother's death."

"Avenge?" asked Sanne softly.

Nicholas nodded. "Keyton said you could help."

"Help how?" Sanne asked.

"I don't know. Talk to the ghost. Then talk to the police."

Angie and Rufus exchanged startled looks. Keyton's eyes went wide.

Sanne reassessed. "Why might I want to talk with the police?"

The red-black on Nicholas flared. His chin lifted. "You're sure asking a lot of questions. I thought you would help." He glanced at Keyton, and raised a hand dismissively as he went to the door. "Forget it."

Nicholas left. Keyton ran after.

For a moment no one spoke.

"Angie," Sanne said softly. "Tell me again how I can't fix everything."

"Hey, Sasquatch!" shouted Keyton, sprinting after the fast-striding Nicholas, who slowed, but only a little, then finally stopped.

Keyton stopped just short. "Fine way to make friends. What the hell are you doing?"

Nicholas didn't turn around. "I'm not the one who ought to be on trial here. Go ask my mother's husband your stupid questions."

"Woah," Keyton said, taken aback, and struggling with what to say next.

Then: "A dangerous business, going out your door, Frodo. Step onto the road, and if you don't keep your feet, someone might say something you don't like."

Nicholas turned around, a fast-vanishing twitch of a smile on his face.

"That's not how it goes."

"Customized for you," Keyton retorted. "Look, I get it: you don't like being challenged. But—" Keyton spread zir hands. "You're involved here. A ghost doesn't just happen. This is about you."

"How do you know that?"

Keyton shrugged. "Seems obvious. It wasn't there before, now it is."

Nicholas rubbed his chin, seeming to be considering.

"I didn't used to get angry so easily," Nicholas admitted.

"Me, neither. It's that red-black stuff."

"The what?"

Keyton heaved a sigh. "Look, there's things you don't know about, but Sanne does. She does magic, the real stuff. She might help you, but you gotta go back in there and not be..." Keyton trailed off.

"An asshole?"

"Yeah, that."

From Nicholas's angry expression, Keyton wondered if he was about to give up and walk away again.

Which was something Keyton understood, that moment where you just bailed.

But now that Keyton knew Nicholas better—knew what he was going through—Keyton realized that ze would not let him go. No matter what.

But also would not hurt him.

"Hey," Keyton said. "I'm sorry I knocked you down on Thursday. And hit you. And called you names. I was a jerk."

"You called me a name like two minutes ago," Nicholas said in a matter-of-fact tone. "Does that mean I get to call you little miss weirdo again?"

Keyton laughed. Couldn't help it. Then Nicholas did, too, and that made Keyton feel good. Even now.

"Yeah, if that's what it takes to get you come back in with me," Keyton said, surprised to mean it.

Funny how fast things could change.

"Real magic, eh?" Nicholas said dubiously. "What, like Gandalf and Saruman?"

Keyton remembered the demon eggs. "Yeah."

Their gazes met. Keyton felt oddly vulnerable in that look, but also kind of happy.

"All right," Nicholas said. "You've turned me from the dark side."

"Doubt that," Keyton said.

Side by side they walked back to Sanne's house.

CHAPTER

TWENTY-TWO

Sanne took in the room. Keyton perched on the edge of the glass coffee table, and was entirely focused on Nicholas.

Things changed fast in teenager land.

Angie sat at one end of the couch, Rufus at the other. Rufus looked at her, but her body language said she wasn't paying any attention to him and never would.

Sanne took a breath and offered the room some brightness, the etheric equivalent of turning up the lights.

Nicholas stood, staring at Sanne as if studying her, making her wonder what Keyton had told him.

"Tell us what you want us to know, Nicholas," Sanne said.

He began to pace the room, his white sneakers landing softly on the pale wood floor.

"In March," he said, "my mother was diagnosed with brain cancer—glioblastoma multiforme. There was surgery, radiation, chemo." He reached the wall, paused, turned, resumed, looking down at his feet. "On August 18th, she didn't come out of her room. My father wouldn't let me see her. Same the next day. The morning after, police and medical showed. Took her out on a stretcher, covered." He reached the other end of the room and stopped at the wall, staring distantly.

No one spoke. No one even twitched.

After a long minute, Nicholas turned again, and resumed his pace. "The medical examiner's report said she died of natural causes. Ischemic stroke."

Silence. Nicholas arrived at the other wall, seemed to shake himself, to remember he had an audience. He turned to face them, his expression bleak.

"Last month, when my father was in the shower, I got a look at her death certificate. It says she died on August 18th. So why did it take until August 20th for police and EMS to come? What happened in the meantime? What the hell?"

"Maybe," Sanne said softly, "he wanted to stay with her a little longer. Some people do."

"Without telling anyone? Without telling me?" He gave Sanne a hurt, incredulous look. His breath was shallow. The red-black energy swirled.

He looked around, found Sanne with his gaze. "I was taught there's no such thing as ghosts. But I don't understand why one picture in twenty on a wall would be off-center every time, even though I set it straight. And what are the noises in the attic? Like storm sounds when there's no storm."

"Or a weather rig camera moving itself on a utility pole." Keyton said.

"What?" Nicholas asked Keyton.

"How I found your house," Keyton said. "I think maybe your grandmother's ghost moved it."

Nicholas's mouth twisted, wryly. Then to Sanne: "Keyton says you're the real thing. Some kind of sorcerer or something. I want to know the truth about how my mother died. What my father did to her. If there's a ghost—if it's my grandmother or whatever—it knows something. Can you ask?"

"Have you tried talking to the ghost?" Sanne asked.

Nicholas's eyebrows drew together. "Don't you have to be—" he waved a hand. "Whatever you are?"

"It's just a skill," Angie said. "You practice. How do you know you can't if you haven't tried?"

Oh, Angie, Sanne thought, *you make me so proud.*

The anger wafted off Nicholas like waves of heat. "I hate him. I want him to pay for whatever he did to her."

Sanne cleared the ripples before they could reach her three. She stood.

"No promises," Sanne said to Nicholas, "But let's see what we can do. First, though..." She turned to look at the three of them. "This is not on any of my lesson plans. You don't have to be here. Anyone want to leave?"

No one did.

"Woah. We're doing this here?" Nicholas asked.

"That's what I had in mind," Sanne said mildly. "Do you have another idea?"

"I thought since the ghost was at my house we'd go there," Nicholas said.

"Distance works differently in spirit," Sanne said. "Not the same physics." An understatement, if everything she'd read about it was any guide.

But who knew? Anyone could write about mysticism. Words were easy.

"Bring out your stones," Sanne said to them, "if it feels right."

"Uhm," Keyton said.

Sanne raised her eyebrows.

"I have Nicholas's. He has mine. Do we need to trade back?"

Was Keyton blushing? Sanne tilted her head slightly. "Ask the stones. I trust you."

"Cool," Keyton said. Then to Nicholas: "Mine says you hang onto mine."

Nicholas frowned at Keyton, then brought out the rough white watermelon tourmaline.

Watermelon tourmaline, a stone that loved to remove barriers and bring together extremes. Perfect.

Sanne moved chairs to clear a central space. It was time to assign work.

"Keyton," Sanne began. "Your job is to stay energy-close to Nicholas. You don't need to be next to him, but I'd like you to make his etherics as contained as possible. You know what I mean?"

"Yeah."

"Angie," Sanne said. "I'm going to be working in the realm of spirit, and so I'll be less able to track us all here. Will you keep things settled in this space, keep the room as clean as you can?"

"Yes, I will."

"Rufus, I'm giving you the job of making and holding the edges, the container the five of us are in. Keep it intact. Keep it company. A bit like the weaving spells we've done. Are you willing?"

"Sure thing."

"Now, let me figure out what I'm doing."

"You don't know?" Nicholas asked.

Sanne gave him an amused look. "Barely a vague plan. If I get too sure of myself, I lose track of what's actually happening. That's a trap." She took in the room, saw that Rufus was already starting to clarify the edges of the space, nodded approval.

"I'll be right back," she said.

In her guest room, she ran fingers over the stones. Each one was in her collection for its properties, but also for its personality, for that rock's particular take on the world. Or worlds.

She wondered, would her mother be proud of what she'd done, of how she'd extended the original set her mother had gifted her when she was nine? Would she like how Sanne had stepped into her mother's work?

"Hope you'd be proud of Marla, too," Sanne whispered to the memory of her mother.

As a lawyer, her sister Marla worked with the perspectives and personalities of humans, a bit like what Sanne did with stones.

Sanne's fingers traveled over the varying stones, bright to muted, smooth or rough, circular, rounded and irregular.

Who wants to help with this? she asked them, then listened.

Four stones responded. Three were unsurprising: a wedge of deep blue lapis lazuli speckled with gold like the stars of the heavens, a finger-length of clear crystal quartz, and an egg shape of forest-green jade.

Then, to her surprise, an orb of red-speckled white cinnabar seemed to raise a cocky finger.

You, too, then. She scooped up the four stones, went back into the living room, where she slowed to sense what they had done in her absence.

Sanne read Nicholas's body language and energy pattern. He was skeptical and impatient. The red-black tightened around him like armor.

Rufus was doing solid work with the edges of the space, and looked like he was having a good time with it. It wasn't that different from what the four of them had done in spring, weaving spells to contain the unexpected delivery of a package of demon eggs, so he'd done it before.

Keyton seemed unsettled, but was keeping the red-black energy from spreading.

And Angie...the room was bright and clear. Angie was right: she could take on more advanced work, and Sanne would not forget that.

Rufus stood at the wall. He was not just defining the edge of the container, he was physically standing on it.

Sanne set her stones on the dark wood floor just inside the circle Rufus was holding, at the four directions of the compass.

"How do I know this isn't just some kind of make-believe?" Nicholas asked.

"Oh, you'll know," Keyton said softly.

"I'm not asking you to believe in anything," Sanne said to Nicholas.

Things were coming together. Nicholas just happened to be

standing roughly at the center of the circle, his doubt ironically serving to anchor the structure that was starting to take form.

Sanne walked the room, just inside the circle. Her energetic fingers touched each stone as she passed. The stones were settling in.

"I guess that's okay, then," Nicholas replied uncertainly. "But you didn't tell me what you want me do."

"I like you just where you are," Sanne replied.

As the four teenagers did their work, Sanne invited the stones to engage. If the stones had been people, they would be turning toward Nicholas as if he were a central campfire, and chattering like friends eager to catch up.

Their conversation was a mutter, an earthy, tumbling rumble, like the hush and splash of a wide river. The cinnabar offered a way down to ground, the lapis a way up to make the space for spirit. Quartz formed a channel. And jade nestled in to build a doorway.

"Will you tell me when it starts?" asked Nicholas in a somewhat timid voice.

Sanne smiled, crossed her legs, and let herself down to sit on the floor by the quartz.

"Nicholas," she said, "would you be willing to tell your grandmother Trinity that we're here, in care and compassion, and if there's something she wants us to know, we're listening?"

Sanne saw Nicholas's breath go shallow, his gaze flickering around the room. His doubt, Sanne assessed, was coming up against something it didn't know quite what to do with.

"You mean out loud?" he asked in a whisper.

"Either way," Sanne answered. "Just ask."

To Sanne's ears, the ones on either side of her head, the room went silent.

To her inner hearing, it was anything but. The mumbling and chuckling of the four stones at the compass points rose in volume. She caught the echoing chatter further out from the stones they each held in hand or pocket, as if the stones were an enthused audience eager for the show to start.

Then, distantly, someone was singing.

Not so distantly. It was coming from her finger.

Thank you, ring. Glad to have you.

"Okay" Nicholas said. "I asked."

But he didn't really need to say so, because Sanne could see Doctor Trinity Mallas just fine.

Sanne gaped. Trinity Mallas stood before her, hand on hip, a pale lab jacket hitched up over a generous skirt, her hair bound loosely in a bun at the back of her head.

Trinity turned to look at Nicholas, her face pinching, quite eloquently expressing her disapproval.

Angie took an audible breath.

Nicholas clearly could not see the ghost, but from his wide eyes and slight trembling lip, Sanne was fairly sure he could feel her.

Keyton and Rufus were frowning, aware something was happening, but not quite sure what.

"Hello, spirit," Sanne said aloud. She felt the four stones she had set at the compass points preening with delight at what had walked through their channel. "Are you Trinity Mallas?"

"Who else?" Trinity turned to face Sanne. "Can you not clear that malevolent slop off of my grandson?"

"Not without understanding it better," Sanne replied. "Can you tell me what it is?"

The ghost seemed suddenly confused, then began to fade.

No, no. Sanne reached out energetic fingers to tap the four stones urgently. *Keep the channel open.*

Of course, Sanne herself was the channel. The stones were partners.

It didn't matter—the ghost was gone as suddenly as she had arrived.

Sanne blinked herself back into the physical, gave an exasperated sigh.

"Was that it? What happened?" Nicholas asked her.

Sanne forced herself to a slow breath, then another, noticing her frustration and how it threatened to take over her thoughts and emotions.

She realized what had happened: she'd offered an open space to a spirit, and then had filled it with her own urgent question, narrowing the scope and making it hard to stay in the fragile channel between spirit and physical.

She stood, aware that she herself teetered on the edge of upset. She could blame herself, and let frustration win, or stay open to what was, and step over the tangle.

"We did good," she said to them with feeling. "All of us. But I made a mistake. She slipped away. I think I know what I did, and what to do better next time." She looked at Nicholas. "I'm sorry. I haven't done this before."

"You haven't? Really?"

"Really," Sanne said.

"Me neither," he said with a fleeting wry smile.

"Do you want to try again?" Sanne asked him.

"Yes."

She looked around the circle. "And the rest of you?"

Everyone nodded.

"All right, then." Sanne again sat again on the floor, feeling beneath and above the house to earth and sky. "This time, Sanne," she muttered to herself, "more listening, less haste."

She nodded at Nicholas, who silently mouthed his invitation.

Again, Rufus described the edges, Angie kept the space, and Keyton held Nicholas.

Trinity Mallas appeared.

She glared at Sanne. "Are you a good witch or a bad witch?"

Sanne's eyebrows shot up in surprise. No fast answers, she reminded herself.

She considered. "I try to be a whole witch."

The answer seemed to satisfy Trinity, who cocked her head at Nicholas. "His father has made a right mess. I want you to clean it up."

"Yes, ma'am," Sanne said.

"I promised my daughter I would be here for her when she passed over to come home. Now I can't, and I don't like breaking my promises. Matthew has to let her go. Make sure of it."

"You mean Gail?" Sanne asked.

Nicholas burst out: "Did he kill my mother? Did my father kill my mother? Ask her!"

"Who else?" Trinity replied to Sanne. Sanne realized Trinity couldn't hear Nicholas any better than he could hear her.

Then Trinity looked confused, and began to fade.

"Doctor Mallas," Sanne said quickly, "did Matthew Gaffon kill Gail?"

"What?" Trinity looked aghast. "Goodness, no. It was an inevitable stroke. Though Matthew loved her enough to royally muck up both of their selves. Now neither can move. Clean this up, witch!"

"Yes, ma'am," Sanne said meekly. "Is there anything else I should know?"

"Your mother is proud of you. And of your sister, too. Make sure she knows."

And Trinity was gone.

CHAPTER

TWENTY-THREE

"Was it her? What did she say?"

Nicholas strode to Sanne, who sat on the floor trying to bring herself back to awareness.

Never having done this before, Sanne hadn't realized how murky and disconnected it would leave her, struggling to come back to her own body.

Also, the ghost's words swept her emotional landscape like a windstorm.

Your mother is proud of you. That meant her mother knew what Sanne had been doing. Had been watching.

"Get up and talk to me," Nicholas shouted down at Sanne.

Rufus came over, and faced Nicholas. "Hey. Ease up."

Sanne felt the container that had held the circle wobble and shatter, felt Keyton lose hold of Nicholas. The air tasted of anger.

Over her, Nicholas addressed Rufus. "You have no idea what it is to lose your mother. So shut the hell up."

Rufus stepped closer, into Nicholas's personal space. The boys were nearly nose to nose.

"But Sanne does," Angie said sharply, cutting through. "She lost both her parents at once."

"You did?" Keyton asked Sanne.

Angie's revelation caught everyone's attention. The moment shifted, the challenge defused.

"I didn't know. When?" Rufus asked.

"I was eleven," Sanne answered numbly.

"You understand then," Nicholas said to Sanne. "Tell me, please, what did she say?"

Sanne got to her feet, unsteadily, then turned to Nicholas.

"Your grandmother told me that your father loved your mother, that your mother died, from an inevitable stroke."

Trinity had said a few other things as well, but right now Sanne judged this to be as much as Nicholas could take.

Nicholas slumped, wrapping his arms around himself, eyes defocusing. Keyton put an arm around him, and led him to the couch to sit.

Angie mouthed to Sanne: "I'm sorry."

Puzzled, it took Sanne a moment. Ah, the revelation of her mother's death. Her secret.

Not really a secret. More like a wound that healed so slowly it was hard to see improvement. A goodbye that had never been said.

Sanne looked at Nicholas, saw the familiar pain, though his was rough and raw.

"It's okay," Sanne said to Angie, determined to make it so.

Sanne hadn't told her teens about her parents' death until now because it had never been relevant to the work she'd been hired to do: tutor them in computer science. And maybe a bit of knitting. Some wildcrafting.

Then, somehow, she was teaching them spellcasting, and how to capture and send baby demons back to their dimension. Not exactly kid stuff.

But they weren't exactly kids.

Across the room, magical structures were breaking apart and dissipating. There was no container, no edge. Emotions roiled.

On the couch, bent over, Nicholas was gulping air, a wordless, silent sobbing. At his side, Keyton looked helpless.

"What do we do now?" Rufus asked softly.

"Lunch, I think," Sanne said.

Plates were full of sandwiches and veggies, cups with water and juice.

Sanne knew that practical action had a way of calming people. Also, major workings had a way of making the body hungry, almost as if it needed to reassert its primacy.

At first Nicholas refused food. But after a while, with the sounds of munching around him, with Keyton silently putting things on his plate, he took a bite. Before long he was consuming a Keyton-decorated sandwich.

When everyone had slowed slightly in their devouring ways, Sanne brought out the remaining cookies they had baked, now a couple of days ago. The memory of that collaboration settled the room further.

"What about the forest?" Rufus asked, glancing meaningfully toward Nicholas.

The other two nodded. So much had happened there. Deep healing. A demon attack that left a gash in the side of one of the great old cedars.

"Nicholas," Sanne said. "What do you want to have happen now?"

"If I can talk to my grandmother, can I talk to my mother? I never got to say goodbye."

It was all Sanne could do to keep her own similar pain off her face.

And apparently, she hadn't. Angie gave her a concerned look.

Sanne put her hand on the table between two plates. There, in the middle of the ring's night-sky-blue stone, the star's six rays were barely nubs around a dim central pale dot.

"I think your mother Gail—some of her, anyway—is stuck in this ring. You can talk to her. But I don't know if she can hear."

Nicholas stared at the ring.

Clean this up, witch!

"And I also think," Sanne said gently, "that we need to get your father involved."

Nicholas's expression went hard.

"Do you think he'd be willing?" Sanne asked.

"No."

"Do you think you could maybe get him closer to being willing?" Sanne tried.

"For my mother? I will try." A pause. He looked at the ring with an expression of longing. "I miss her so much. She was a great mom."

"Tell us about her," Sanne invited.

Nods from all around. "Tell us," Rufus said.

"We'd like to know," Angie said.

"But only if you want to say," Keyton added.

Nicholas looked around the table.

He sniffled. "Yeah, I'd like that." He took a deep breath. "This one time, when I was five..."

CHAPTER
TWENTY-FOUR

The next morning was blustery, light puffs of air promising a storm.

With any luck. Sanne could stand some wind and rain. A bit of nature's own housekeeping.

Sanne walked the forest trail toward her grove of old growth cedars. A few red and yellow leaves of maples and alders still hung, waving in the breeze.

Before he left her house yesterday, Sanne had given Nicholas some ideas about how he might get his father to join them.

Matthew, said the ring, as if reading her mind.

Sanne wrapped her other hand around the ring, sending it care. A hand hug.

Sadness wafted from the ring.

Sanne dropped her shoes and socks. Her feet bare and callused, she walked the dirt and loam, making a wide circle around the three great cedars. Nettle brushed the sides of her ankles, offering the plant's tingling tonic.

Just two seasons ago she and her three students—and Della, too—had saved these very trees from developers, and they had done that by looking at the problem from an entirely different angle. And some magic.

How you looked at a problem made all the difference.

Sanne touched the ground in the four directions, calling in the compass points and their powers on this cool autumn day. Aloud she named the tribes who had once lived here and called it home.

Then she gave a greeting to the three ancient trees.

Welcome, the trees replied.

Never an ordinary moment, hearing centuries-old trees speak to her.

May I approach? And my friends, when they arrive?

Yes and welcome.

She stepped over roots snaking across the ground, the corded trunk rising up and up, branches far above reaching to the sky.

She put her hands on the bark, setting the ring against the wood.

Touch. Breath. Kiss. The bark tasted of life and death, of the connectedness of the forest. Of circles and time.

She sat, putting her back to the tree, and looked up through evergreens to patches of sky, white, then blue, and then white again.

"Hello."

Angie, at the edge of the clearing. Right on time.

Sanne smiled, and gestured for Angie to join her. Angie took off her shoes—something Sanne had never told any of them to do, but which they did anyway.

Angie joined Sanne, and sat.

She felt Angie tense as Rufus entered the clearing. He sat on Sanne's other side, facing Angie.

Keyton, arriving last, dropped shoes and socks alongside the others, and sat across from Sanne, completing the circle.

"We have an opportunity today," Sanne said, "to help Nicholas and his father to sort things out, with each other, and with the loss of someone they loved very much. Do you want to help with that?"

"Sure thing," said Rufus.

"I do," said Angie.

"Of course," said Keyton. "Why are you even asking?"

"Because it might not be so easy for them to do this work," Sanne said. "In order for us to help them—to make the right space for them—we're going to need to be as clear in ourselves as we hope they can be. So: are we willing to clean up what's happened between us? Which also might not be so easy?"

There it was: silence, unmet gazes, tightness.

No surprise.

Sanne reached into the side pocket of her jacket, brought out a silvery lump of hematite, weighty in her hand. One side was faceted and smooth, the other bumpy and rough. It was a beautiful piece, holding in its different parts both clarity and confusion, the aspirational and the pragmatic.

"You don't have to," Sanne added. "Consider how you want to be part of this, today."

Then she raised her left hand, the one with the ring. "I'm in this, too. I'll do the work with you. I'm not an observer."

"Okay," Angie said decisively.

"Yeah," Rufus replied.

Keyton took a deep breath, let it out slowly. "I'm in."

Pride and something else washed through her. A bit of fear, perhaps. Because you couldn't talk truth without risking changing things.

But then, things would change anyway. It was just a matter of direction.

"Here we go, then," Sanne said. She tossed the hematite rock into the center between the four of them. It landed with a soft sound on fallen leaves and dirt. "Hematite for grounding. Do you feel it?"

They all nodded, Rufus hesitantly.

Sanne took from her jacket a long wand of milky white.

"This is a selenite wand," Sanne said. "It'll be our talking stick. When someone holds it, we resolve to give them our best, most heartfelt listening. But it's not a conversation. If you hold the stick, you can speak. Or not. If you speak, honor your listeners by speaking your truth, from the heart, less from the head. Do you remember the anger class, and how to use I-statements?"

They all nodded.

"Pick something to say," Sanne said. "Maybe a level two or three of intensity, but not all the way to ten. When you're done, give the stick to the next person. You don't need to say everything —we'll keep going until no one has more."

"What if I'm not ready?" asked Angie.

"Just say 'pass'. We'll come back to you." Sanne looked around to make sure everyone understood.

"I'll start." Sanne took a breath, and searched her emotions. "You're all changing," she said, turning the cool wand over in her hands. "So fast. That's as it should be—it's your primary job, at this age. But there's a part of me that's afraid to lose you as you are." She looked at the hematite at the center. "Afraid to lose some of you for good. But that's no gift to you, nor to me. So I want to do better at letting you become and not hold you back. I resolve to keep that in my mind and heart."

Sanne's eyes stung. Was this what parents felt about their own children?

She gave this a moment, letting them absorb her words. She passed the wand to her right.

Angie took it, holding it in both her upturned palms.

"Pass," she said, and handed it to Keyton.

Keyton twitched in surprise, accepted the stick, and balanced it horizontally between the webbing of both of zir hands, tilting it back and forth.

Keyton asked Sanne: "What if we all pass?"

"Then you'll learn a lot about me," Sanne said with a light smile.

"Pass," Keyton said softly, handing the wand to Rufus.

"Pass," Rufus said at once, offering the wand to Sanne. Then: "Wait. No. Blast it." Rufus took back the wand, holding it in his left hand, glaring at it.

He scrambled to his feet, looked around at each person, gaze lingering on Angie, and turned to Keyton.

"You said you hit me because I got in your way. I don't think that's a good reason. Now, every time I talk to you, I worry you'll be mad, so I don't say anything at all." He shrugged. "It's not so much being hit that bugs me. It's that I want our friendship back. To be able to talk to you." He pondered a moment. "Though I'd also like it if you didn't hit me, too."

Keyton's eyes went as wide as they could go.

So much for not picking a level-ten issue, Sanne thought, and reminded herself to breathe.

Rufus thunked himself back down on the ground, hunched forward over his crossed legs. After a moment he seemed to recall that he was still holding the selenite stick and handed it to Sanne.

Not children any more, she reminded herself.

"Let's keep going," Sanne said, leaning into her belief that they could handle this, that the circle could hold what arose. "We'll give those who passed a chance to speak if they want to. You don't have to. Angie?"

"Pass again," Angie said, taking the wand and handing it to Keyton.

Keyton gripped the milky white wand at its center, rotating it back and forth in an arc.

At the edge of the clearing a squirrel chittered. Branches rattled as it jumped from one bare alder branch to another.

Keyton's gaze was on the hematite rock in the center. "Thing is…" Keyton gave an exasperated sigh. "I am sorry." A moment passed. "Yeah, I hit Rufus. And Nicholas. And probably Angie, too. I'm not even sure, and how stupid is that? I don't feel good about it. But I also don't know how to make it right." Keyton's mouth and eyes twisted down as if trying not to cry. "If I knew how, I'd do it."

Sanne saw the surprise and empathy of the other two, their gaze on Keyton.

Keyton reached over the hematite stone, offering the wand to Sanne. "Who gets it next?"

"Angie," Sanne answered, gesturing the wand to the side. "Though she can pass again."

"No, I'll take it," Angie said, accepting the wand from Keyton. She glanced at Sanne. "Speak from my heart, you said. Okay. Yesterday, when you lost Trinity's ghost, before you got her back, you said that you had made a mistake. I keep thinking about that. How you said it. Like it was okay to make mistakes, and then to come back and try things again, with what you learned. That's how I want to be. So, I might not say this right, but here goes."

Angie looked at Sanne, then to the silvery center stone. "When I told you Sunday that I wanted to leave the group, I think that was a mistake, because I wanted to not deal with the hard stuff." She looked at Keyton. "I can forgive you for hitting me. And also for saying mean things. If you can do what Sanne did, or at least try."

Angie gave a decisive nod, then sat back down. "We all went. Do we start over now?"

"Yes," Sanne said, accepting the stick back. "Let's go the other way this time. I'll go last. Remember, it's okay to pass, or even take your turn and say nothing, just letting us give you our best attention." She offered the wand to Rufus.

He looked around at the group, then at the hematite stone. In the long minute that followed, the wind picked up, trees rustling leaves, and high branches of the ancient trees creaking overhead.

"I think I have a crush on Angie," he said.

"You do not," Angie snapped, standing abruptly.

Rufus looked up at her, his mouth agape at the reaction. "I said I think."

"Angie," Sanne said. "Would you be willing to let Rufus finish? You'll have a turn, I promise. And when it's you, we'll all give you our best, most caring attention."

Angie's face was full of outrage. She sat again, crossed her arms, and snorted.

"Rufus," Sanne said, "Speaking for myself anyway, I'm still here and listening. Is there more you want to say?"

"Well," Rufus said slowly, "I guess since I've already pissed her off, which sucks, and she's thinking of leaving the group, which sucks even more, I should just say the rest." He took a breath, looked at Sanne. "I don't think I'm smart enough for her, you know? And my family's said some racist stuff before, and she knows that, and that sucks, too. But I like her. A lot. I keep thinking, what if I asked her out? Would she laugh at me? Then I think, no, Angie isn't like that. Then I think, you're a coward if you can't even ask. And you know what? I am." He pushed out his lower jaw, as if daring anyone to disagree.

No one spoke.

"Or, maybe, I was," Rufus said. He took a deep breath, then got to his feet and looked at Angie.

"Angie," he said, "I'm sorry for being dense sometimes. Maybe I could try harder, or pay better attention. Or maybe I'm just dense. But I really like you."

Overhead, a red-tailed hawk gave a long, thready call. Rufus looked up at the sound. "I think I'd rather know for sure than always wonder if she would have gone on a date with me if I'd asked." His gaze went back to Angie, who scowled at him.

His expression changed as he stepped into courage. Sanne felt the quality of the circle change. "So," Rufus said to Angie, "I'm asking."

Sanne felt chills run up and down her. Rufus sat down on the ground again, looking entirely unnerved by his own actions, but also like someone who had, in this last minute, had an impressive emotional growth spurt.

And Angie, well...her energy field was a jagged thicket, her face and body showing anger and shock.

Sanne fed energy into grounding the center and connecting them all to the stone. It helped, but only a little, flooded as it was with high-intensity waves of emotion and energy.

Rufus handed the wand to Keyton, who took it rather more calmly than last time.

"I've been angry a lot lately," Keyton said. "That's not an excuse, but here's the thing: I see a lot of anger at home. My parents fight. All the time. They're probably getting divorced. I hate that."

For a moment, Keyton's breath was fast and shallow. Then Keyton slowed it, with focus.

Around the circle, the other two mirrored Keyton's breath. Slow in, slow out.

"I want to do what you said, Angie," Keyton continued. "What Sanne does. I'm not sure I know how. I might need help. Rufus, I want you to trust me again. Also, I have a crush on Nicholas, since we're on that stuff."

No one looked the least bit surprised.

Keyton blushed and handed the wand to Angie.

Angie snorted, glared at Rufus, snorted again. She gripped the wand tightly at one end, rolled up onto her legging-clad knees, and stabbed the wand toward Rufus, then did it again.

"All right, look," she said finally. "You said 'Hell no,' when—" she pointed the wand at Keyton. "—when Nicholas asked—" Again, she poked toward Rufus. "—'this one your girlfriend?' Remember that?"

"Angie," Sanne interjected gently while holding a hand toward Rufus, who was bouncing and clearly wanted to respond. "It's not a conversation. Are you speaking from your heart?"

"No, damnit," Angie said, and rolled to the side to sit on the ground. She put the selenite stick flat against the skin of her forehead, and shut her eyes. "Let me try again." She opened her eyes. "When I heard him say that, it hurt, because I thought he meant he would be disgusted to even think it, because I'm Black."

As Angie said the last phrase, Rufus began adamantly shaking his head. He continued the motion as if he would never get tired of it.

Angie watched, her expression changing from anger to bewilderment. "Then what did you mean?" Angie asked.

Rufus sighed heavily, his expression conveying remorse. Angie frowned.

Sanne decided it was the right moment to make an exception. She addressed Rufus. "Go ahead. Keep it brief."

"I was scared," Rufus said to Angie, his voice small. "To like you that much."

"Oh," Angie said, and Sanne could see her putting the pieces together as she reassessed Rufus. The energy in the circle shifted again. Then: "Okay, I'm going to need to think about that."

Angie handed the wand to Sanne.

Sanne rolled it between her palms, letting the silence lengthen and encouraging the two stones—the silvery hematite in the center and the selenite in her hands—to settle what had just flared.

"About my parents," Sanne said. "I was eleven when they died." She made eye contact with each of them, making sure to ground herself and her grief deep into the earth, refusing to let them hold any of it.

She thought of Jerry who had become their guardian. What a tangled, antagonistic relationship that had been, though the letter he'd left helped.

"It's still not easy," Sanne admitted. "But I am who I am because of everything that's happened to me, which includes that." Sanne felt the tree at her back, like an old friend, helping to keep her in the moment.

With the wand in her right hand, she held out her left to examine the ring. "I want to help this ring and the spirit in it find its way home. I want to give Nicholas and his father the faith that they can come through this hard time. That it's possible. Because I have."

She looked around the circle.

She judged that they had probably done as much as they would do today, and should wrap up. Maybe ask Keyton to text

Nicholas to see how he was doing with the project of getting his father to join them.

They were her kids, she decided. But not kids for much longer.

"Another round," she said decisively. "For myself I feel done, for today. But you don't have to be. If you feel done, say pass. If not, speak and we will hear you."

One by one, they passed. Even Rufus, who seemed to feel that he had said enough.

The wand came back to Sanne. "Thank you all for your courage. For your heart." She reached her hands out to either side. The four of them linked hands, and Sanne spoke a spell to honor the work and release the container they had made.

She let them go. Smiled at each, and looked at Keyton. "Anything from Nicholas?"

Keyton took out zir phone.

"On his way. I'll walk back to the street, show them where to park. Walk them in."

"Both?"

Keyton nodded, typing on the phone. "I texted: how did you manage to convince him to come?"

"What did he say?" asked Angie.

Keyton waited for a reply.

"'I just told him everything,'" Keyton quoted.

TWENTY-FIVE

What was everything?

What, Sanne wondered, would Matthew Gaffon make of hearing that the ghost of his mother-in-law had come back to answer questions about his recently deceased wife and assure his son that Matthew wasn't a murderer?

Sanne met Nicholas and Matthew as they stepped out of the brush at the edge of the clearing.

"Oh, it's you," Matthew said to Sanne, recognizing her. "Nick called you something else."

"My friend-name is Sanne," Sanne said, looking up at the tall Matthew Gaffon. "Use it if you wish."

She offered her hand. Matthew took it. His grip was surprisingly mild.

As they released their touch, Sanne brushed off some of the red-black ooze that had tried to crawl up her arm.

"She came to our house," Matthew explained to Nicholas. "To talk to you. I told her to go away. I was, perhaps, not at my best."

Sanne asked the four teenagers if they'd give her and Matthew time to talk. The teens tromped over twigs and through brush, then out of sight.

Matthew said, "Looks like he might have made a friend. I'm glad."

Here, where forest life circled and intertwined with the great, ancient trees, the red-black cloud around Matthew swirled more slowly.

"She used to say," Matthew said, "there's way more that we don't know than we do, so stay humble."

"You mean Gail?" asked Sanne.

Matthew nodded, hooking his thumbs through the belt loops of his jeans, and shifting his weight from one leg to the other. "She got the adage from her mother." He looked around. "These are some big trees."

"Hundreds of years old. Probably on the order of five hundred."

"Gail was only forty-seven."

"I'm sorry."

"Nicholas told me you talked to my mother-in-law, Trinity. That you're a medium."

Sometimes a large, Sanne thought, but caught the quip before it found its way to her mouth.

"Not quite," she said, searching for a way to explain. "It's not my area, talking to the dead, but I come from a family line where ghosts were considered part of life. I suppose my ancestors could have been called witches," she said cautiously.

"Mine, too," he said, which Sanne wasn't expecting. "Though by the time I knew enough to ask him for details, my father insisted he was done with all that, and then refused to say more."

The pieces started to fit.

"So when Gail died..." she said.

He grimaced, turned his head away.

"She was still there," he whispered fiercely. "I could feel her. I thought if I could hold her, get her back into her body, her eyes would open. I could tell her how much I loved her."

The red-black smoke pulsed around him.

"She was dead?"

"It was so fast. Medically, nothing I could do. But I've seen people come back from a stroke, open their eyes, and ask what happened." His voice dropped. "Gail should have had months more. All I had to do was keep her there. I tried and tried, but it didn't work."

He didn't know what he had done. This wasn't the first time Sanne had met someone who could wield power but didn't realize it.

They were among the most dangerous.

"It did work, though," Sanne said gently. "You stopped her from leaving." She held up her left hand. "Part of her went into this."

"Into her ring? Nicholas's ring?"

Sanne nodded. "I think she's somewhere else, too. She's in parts."

"That what your ghost told you?" Matthew asked with a cynical smirk that reminded Sanne of Nicholas.

"You don't need to believe me," Sanne said mildly.

He eyed the silver ring. "You going to return that to us?"

"Be happy to. As soon as I can take it off." Sanne pulled at it fruitlessly, then held out her hand to Matthew, who also tugged at it without effect.

"Soap and water," he suggested.

Sanne gave a short laugh. "Not that kind of stuck."

"Explain."

"Hello," Sanne whispered to the ring on her finger. "What do you need now?"

Matthew.

She looked up at Matthew. "The ring is asking for you. She wants you, but she can't find you."

For a moment, Matthew's expression broke and Sanne saw his grief. She held out her hand, and he put his thumb on the night-blue star sapphire, his forefinger curled under the band.

"I'm right here," he said to the ring, voice hoarse.

Matthew, wailed the ring.

His eyes tightened. Had he heard it, too?

Then he withdrew his hand, expression hardening. "Nicholas believes you. But he's thirteen."

"Then why did you come here today?" she asked gently.

"I'm out of leave. I have to go back to work. I can't find a reason to care, except for my son. When Nicholas told me that until your seance yesterday he'd been thinking I might have killed his mother, I realized how bad things had gotten." He lifted his chin. "He said you might know what to do."

Way more that we don't know than we do, so stay humble.

"I'll give it my best," she replied.

"You talked to Trinity?" he asked. "Really?"

"I think so. Hair in a bun, wearing a lab coat? Acts like she's in charge?"

Matthew gave a bark of surprised laughter. It had a rusty sound to it, as if it hadn't been used in a while.

"Sounds like her, all right. She wanted Gail to marry a doctor, not some lowly EMT. Took years for her to warm up to me. She finally did. What did she say?"

"She said: you need to let Gail go."

The red-black around Matthew thickened, dissipated, and thickened again. A hummingbird whirred past them both, a flicker of iridescent green.

Matthew looked past Sanne at the great trees. The silence stretched.

"I like this place," he said after a bit. "Gail would have, too." He exhaled slowly. "I'm terrible at asking for help."

"Offer you some advice?" Sanne asked quietly.

"Yeah."

"I think the very best expert we have on what to do next," Sanne said, "is you."

His head jerked back to look at her. "Me? I didn't know what I was doing when I tried to keep her alive. How would I know now?"

"What you did was a spell. Consciously or not, you knew

enough to make it. Consciously or not, you know enough to unmake it."

"You mean let her go."

Sanne nodded.

Matthew's expression dissolved into raw emotion. "You're asking me to change everything."

Sanne held up her left hand. "It's not me asking."

The four teens hovered at the far end of the clearing. Sanne gestured to them to come back.

As leaves and twigs crunched under their feet, Sanne said to Matthew, "You'll have all our support if you want it. Though I might suggest you start by talking to the trees."

"The trees?"

"Yes. Just put your hands on the bark. Ask anything. Listen, just in case they answer."

Matthew grunted once, then strode across the clearing to the three trees, reaching the center one, with the gash from the demon attack.

Matthew's open hands hesitated before they touched the bark. Sanne could guess that he sensed this was the point of no return, and after this, what he had done—what he had put all his energy into over those three days—to keep his beloved Gail— would be undone.

Sanne understood how agonizingly hard this moment could be.

The four teens came to Sanne's side.

The moment Matthew put his palms flat on the dark, corded bark, it began.

The red-black cloud thickened, then thinned, and began to flow like water down Matthew's legs and into the ground. It ran along his arms to the tree trunk. It surged up through his chest and neck. Where his forehead touched the tree, it streamed into the bark.

"He's moving the red-black stuff, isn't he?" Angie asked Sanne.

"He is," Sanne said. "The trees are helping."

Distantly, an eagle called a high, long note.

Sanne felt it then, the eddy and cascade of time and space, of doors opening.

"Who's got their stones?" she whispered. All four reached into pockets and brought out what Sanne had lent them.

Without speaking, Keyton and Nicholas swapped stones back. Angie held out her amethyst and obsidian, Rufus his carnelian and mookaite.

Sanne let herself down to the ground, digging her fingers into the dirt. The others joined her. She noticed how easily Nicholas slid into the circle.

Her sense was that Matthew was about as far as he could go by himself. Despite the ring on her finger—which might be there a long time if things didn't get sorted out today—this whole process was up to him. But she could arrange things, in case he wanted help.

"Let's make a compass," she said softly. She pointed. "That's north. Pick a direction, and put yourself on a compass point. You're not just taking a position, you're taking a position in a constellation with each other. If someone else is already in your spot, that's okay. Decide together who takes the point, and who moves. Where you are isn't as important as how you decide together."

"Me, too?" asked Nicholas.

Sanne nodded.

They all stood. Wordlessly they began to sort themselves out, circling Sanne, who kept her gaze on Matthew.

The red-black energy had largely faded from his field. Faded, but still there.

The group settled out: Nicholas north, Angie east, Rufus south, and Keyton west.

In the work of arranging themselves, they had decluttered the remaining energy shards and tangles between them. It would all shift again, of course, but for the moment, they had woven themselves into a whole. Which was the point.

At the center, Sanne felt the space clear, and sweet, as if she were floating in a clean pool of spring water.

Matthew turned to put his back to the wide tree. After a moment, he walked back.

"I unmade it as well as I could manage," Matthew said to her. "But I don't think it's done."

Sanne tugged on the ring, which didn't budge. "Nope."

"I'll take some more help if you're offering," Matthew said.

The circle of four shuffled sideways, staying in their constellation, to put Sanne and Matthew at the center.

"I don't think I should be in the middle," Sanne said.

"Yes, you should," Angie said. "You've got the ring."

"Oh, yes," Sanne said. She felt something, a shift she couldn't quite name. Then she could: she wasn't in charge. These four had just taken on navigation.

Following Angie's lead, the four teenagers opened their hands and put their stones at their feet.

Sanne reached into her pocket, and brought out two more stones: an lustrous green-blue labradorite, and a glossy black egg of shungite.

"You might like this one," she said, offering Matthew the shungite.

He weighed it in one hand, considering. As he did, the remaining red-black fell from his hand like flakes of char.

"Yep," he said, nodding.

Sanne cradled the labradorite and the ring in her left hand.

"You okay?" she asked the ring softly.

Matthew, it replied. Then: *Nicholas.*

"Soon, I hope," Sanne.

Then, to her surprise, Matthew wrapped his larger hand around her hand, the one clutching the ring and green-blue labradorite.

Sanne felt it at once: another presence, hovering and circling, with passion, with love.

She could nearly see it, the figure that stopped in front of Matthew and put a handless-hand to his face, ghostly lips to his.

Matthew closed his eyes, tears streaming.

"I'm sorry, babe," he whispered.

No, never. I love you. Sanne heard from the realm of spirit.

"Nicholas," Matthew said, reaching his other hand toward his son.

Nicholas hesitated.

"Go, go," said Angie, moving to take the north position.

"We've got this," Keyton whispered to him.

Nicholas and Matthew linked hands.

"Oh, I can almost see her," Nicholas breathed.

The spirit drifted to Nicholas and engulfed him in an embrace.

I love you, Sanne heard the spirit say to Nicholas. Then *I love you,* to Matthew. *I will be here for you when you're ready to come home.*

Another ghostly whisper followed, softly, in Sanne's ear: *Thank you.*

Then, though it had no face—no forward side, no backward side—Sanne sensed it turn away.

On the ground, leaves circled and spiraled upward, then settled down again. There stood Trinity in her lab coat.

The spirit of Gail reached for her mother Trinity, who reached back. Handless, yet hand in hand, they stepped through a doorway that was somehow both there and not there.

As they passed through, they paused to look back, smiled, and were gone.

Sanne's eyes were wet as she watched, in frank astonishment.

The empty doorway shimmered. Then another face without a face came to the edge of that doorway.

Finding Sanne's gaze, she smiled. *So proud, Baby,* she said.

"Mom," Sanne mouthed.
The doorway was gone.

TWENTY-SIX

The ring slid off Sanne's finger and dropped to the earth. She picked it up and offered it to Nicholas.

He held the silver ring out on his palm. "Too small for me to wear. I've tried."

"If you want," Matthew said, "I'll get you a chain so you can wear it around your neck."

"That would be great, Dad. Oh, look: the star is gone." Nicholas held the ring to show the night-blue of the stone, now featureless.

"She's free," Sanne said, "Though I wouldn't be surprised if the star came back now and then."

Nicholas curled his hand around the ring, staring distantly.

"So?" asked Matthew slowly, turning to look at each of them and landing his gaze on Sanne. "Is it done?"

Sanne could reply to him that Matthew and Nicholas were clear of the red-black energy, that the spirit in the ring—and the ring—had both found their way home.

She could also say that she'd guess their house would be more quiet, but that they might feel Trinity around from time to time.

And she could answer that Matthew and Nicholas, too, were

now free. Free to begin their healing journey through the rocky lands of grief, an uneven path for which there was no map.

So many words. Sanne knew from her own journey through those hard, rocky lands that sometimes words didn't help a bit.

Everyone was looking at her. She looked back, silently sending a gentle healing wave to Matthew and Nicholas.

A rustle in the brush caught her eye. A small animal took to flight, a shape flitting high into the branches of an alder. There it perched to sing the flute-like trill of a wren.

A family bird, the small, brown wren. A community bird. A nest-builder who would share its home with strangers when the weather got cold.

A good omen, if they needed one.

"I think the red-black stuff is gone," Angie said, looking with a soft gaze at Matthew.

"Yeah. I don't see it either," Keyton agreed.

"I'm not sure I ever saw it," muttered Rufus.

"Sometimes it's not exactly visual," Angie told Rufus. "More like an impression. Or, maybe for you, it's something you can taste."

"Oh, I see," Rufus said, all at once excited. His tongue flickered out and back as if he were tasting the air.

Matthew looked exhausted, like someone who had just begun to come back to health after a dire illness.

"I want to take my son home," Matthew said. "I'm grateful to you all. Especially you, Sanne, for facing me when I was at my worst, but then giving me a chance to be at my best."

"We're all about giving chances around here," Sanne replied. "And glad to be able to help you."

Her three teenagers nodded.

"Sometime soon," Matthew said, "maybe I can thank you all, somehow."

"I like ice cream," said Keyton.

Angie snorted.

Rufus brightened. "You could take us to Poly's Parlor in

Cottonwood Creek. The website says Poly started making black sesame last week. Perfect combo with the cod."

"Cod, as in fish? Fish ice cream?" asked Nicholas, his reaction a mix of fascination and revulsion.

"He loves weird food," Angie said.

"Sure I do," Rufus replied to her, "but *you* might like the new cherry apricot cardamom."

"Oh," Angie said, looking intrigued and pleased. "I might."

"And me?" Keyton asked Rufus. "What would I like?"

Rufus tilted his head. "Rhubarb-rosemary and mint," Rufus answered.

Keyton said, "Oh, yeah, I'm in."

"I'm sure there's somewhere I can get coffee," said Sanne.

"Hang on," Rufus said, clearly delighted with this challenge, "How about Poly's new chocolate, ancho pepper, and lime?"

Sanne's eyebrows rose. "How did you know I like..."

"Settled, then," Matthew said. "I'll take you all to Cottonwood for Poly's."

Overhead, the sky thundered. In moments rain followed.

Perfect timing, Sanne thought. She didn't even mind that by the time she got home, she was soaked to the skin.

TWENTY-SEVEN

"Daddy," Angie said, sitting herself on the pale pink living area couch. "I worked it out with my friends, about the fight."

"Of course you did," her father said. She peered at his laptop on the coffee table. He was scrolling through emails.

"I want to ask you something," she said.

"Go," he said.

"I'd ask mom," said Angie, "but you're a boy."

That earned her a quick glance, and a hint of a frown.

"Not last I checked. This is about a boy?"

"Yes."

"The answer is no," her father said, continuing to scroll.

"You don't even know the question yet," Angie replied.

"No boys. Not until you're thirty."

"Howard," called Angie's mother warningly from the far end of the room, where she sat at a desk with her own laptop.

"Your mother doesn't like my answer."

"I don't either," said Angie.

"Okay. You're unusually mature. Twenty-five."

"Howard," her mother called again.

"That's as low as I'm going, love," he called back.

Angie drew in a breath. "A friend asked me out on a date."

"No."

"That's not what I'm asking," Angie replied. "Mom!"

"Howard."

"Boys are evil," her father said.

Angie rolled her eyes. "Even you?"

"Especially him," said her mother.

"Mom, you're not helping. Dad, Listen. There's a boy, and I think I might like him, but I'm not sure. I don't want to lead him on. But how do I find out, if I can't say yes to a date? How do I reverse things if I decide I don't like him that way? Won't he be hurt?"

Her father stopped scrolling, and slowly shut the lid of his laptop.

"You're only fourteen. Too early to date."

"Do you want to see my meta-analysis showing that I'm actually exactly average for my age, parents, their education, and other demographics?"

"Why am I not surprised," he said. "How old is he?"

"My age."

"He's too young."

Angie gave him a fierce scowl.

He briefly winced. "Does he listen? When you speak?"

Angie nodded.

"Is he kind? Does he treat his friends well?"

"Yes."

"All right, twenty-one."

"Dad!"

Her father turned to face her on the couch, one leg bent. He put a hand on his dark knit pants, and his expression turned serious.

"My dearest daughter—"

"Your only daughter," Angie replied dryly.

"As far as you know."

"Howard," called her mother again.

"My only daughter," her father began again. "You can't derive these answers from a spreadsheet. You can't know before you embark. You have to take the risk."

"Preach," her mother said.

"And even after you take the risk, you won't know."

"Preach again," her mother said.

"Heck, it was only last year that I realized that I liked your mother that way."

Her mother laughed. "Howard," she chided, but it was softened by her continued chuckling.

"Dad, I don't want to lose him as a friend if it turns out that I don't feel that way about him."

"I get you. But romance isn't safe." His eyes flickered across the room toward Angie's mother who looked back. For a moment, their gazes met, their expressions sober. Tender.

"I might lose him as a friend, you're saying." Angie said.

"You might. Or you might not. Or you might gain something really special beyond friendship."

"You're an engineer, dad. I thought you'd have a clearer answer," Angie said.

"Is he as smart as you are?" asked her father.

"That's a hard one," Angie said slowly. "I think maybe he's differently smart."

"That's diplomatic of you," her father said. "So he's not, then. You can date him when you're twenty-one."

"Dad."

"Howard."

Her father took her hand. "In all seriousness, dearest of my many possible daughters, if you like him well enough to wade through your old man's humor to ask advice, the kid might have something going for him. If he hurts you, though, I will kill him."

Angie sighed. "This is the part where you're serious?"

He took her other hand, holding both of her hands in his. "You're intelligent, you're sensible, and you're fourteen. You're going to make some mistakes."

"I don't want him to be one of them."

"Best of luck with that." Her father returned her hands to her, patted her knee, and opened his laptop again. "All in a day's work. What a great dad," he said.

Angie rolled her eyes. "You know, some people have parents who don't joke all the time."

"Who? We'll send a sympathy card," her father said.

Angie got up, walked over to her mother. "Mom?"

"I'm not even sure I like your father that way yet," her mother said.

"Mom," Angie said. "Don't you have any advice?"

Her mother reached out, put her hands on Angie's shoulders, and looked her in the eye. "Angela, darling, you are smart, kind, and wise. I trust you. Trust yourself."

"Trust myself to make mistakes and learn from them, you mean?" Angie asked.

"There you go. Wise, too."

"And if I hurt him? If I get hurt?"

Her mother's face turned sad. "Then you're alive. But if you don't take the risk, you'll never know."

CHAPTER

TWENTY-EIGHT

"High school next year," Nicholas said.

Keyton kicked zir heels gently against the planter box outside the library.

The two of them sat together on the edge again.

Nicholas had texted, and Keyton had shown up.

Keyton wondered: was this a date? And if so, what made it one? It was all very confusing.

"Hope we go to the same one," Keyton said.

"We will," Nicholas said, staring into the distance.

"How can you be so sure?"

He exhaled a laugh. "After what I've been through, that'll be easy." He gave Keyton a glance. "Also, there's only one public high school in town. Anyway, I have a bigger problem."

"What?"

"The June middle school prom. People are going to dress up, and it'll be stupid and silly, and I don't have anyone to go with."

Keyton felt a lot of things all at once, and finally understood the butterflies-in-stomach thing. Yep, that was exactly what it felt like.

"I think I could help with that," Keyton managed, without zir voice wavering too much.

"Yeah?"

"But you might not like it."

"Because?"

"Because what are you going to wear?"

"A tux. I wore a tux to big-wig doctor events with my mother. I look good in it."

Keyton just bet he did.

"Because I'm not going to wear a stupid prom dress," Keyton said.

"Oh," Nicholas said, drawing the word out slowly.

Keyton swallowed hard. Maybe ze would wear one. Was it that big a deal?

Yeah, ze decided, it was.

"I'm sure you can find someone else," Keyton said.

Keyton counted the wordless seconds that followed. One, two, and then uncomfortably many.

"But I don't want someone else," Nicholas said.

Keyton felt a tremble in the throat and a ripple of relief.

"So, okay. What would you wear?" asked Nicholas.

Keyton's chin lifted. "Maybe a tux. Maybe something else. I don't know."

"Not what you're wearing now, though."

"No."

"Okay," Nicholas said. "But something fancy?"

"You want fancy?" Keyton asked.

"Yeah."

"Okay, something fancy," Keyton said.

"Can I pin a flower on it?"

"Yeah," Keyton said.

"All right. I can live with that. You're going with me to the prom, then."

Keyton felt chills. "Okay."

"I got another question," said Nicholas.

"Shoot."

"If you're going to prom with me, then I have to call you

something in the meantime. Like I always figured it would be 'girlfriend'. But I bet you don't want that. What do I call you?"

What do I call you?

All at once Keyton felt giddy, like a kid at a candy shop window, with a topped-up debit card in hand.

Only the candy was Nicholas and how he looked at zir. Because it wasn't every day that a guy as pretty as Nicholas asked Keyton what term of affection ze might want.

Keyton grinned wide. "English sucks."

"Yeah it does. And?"

"You could call me your they-friend."

"Okay."

"You don't like it?"

Nicholas shrugged. "If that's what you want. Let's say I'm bringing you home for dinner to meet my dad and..."

To meet my dad. Keyton could hardly sit still.

"I already met your dad."

"Yeah, in the forest, doing big crazy magic stuff. Not for dinner. Zefriend?" Nicholas asked.

"I'd be okay with Zefriend," Keyton said.

"Yah?" Nicholas was looking at Keyton now. "Hey, are you blushing?"

"No, shut up. I'm thinking."

Nicholas laughed softly, but now Keyton knew it was nothing like mocking, because that's not how he was.

"Boo," Keyton said.

"Like a ghost?"

"No. Like my boo, or boo-friend. I think it's sweet. We could try it. Maybe I could call you that, too." Keyton's face felt warm.

Nicholas mouthed the words, then nodded. "Okay, boo-friend."

On the cement planter between where they sat, Nicholas moved his hand closer to Keyton's, and Keyton's moved closer, too.

Later, Keyton would lie in bed and replay this moment, trying to decide if they both really did move their hands simultaneously to reach each other.

Fingers entwined. Hands met. It felt amazing.

Keyton couldn't imagine anything better. Even the rhubarb-rosemary and mint ice cream, which had been moderately fantastic. Zir heart was beating very fast.

"There's nothing like looking if you want to find something," Nicholas said in a forced deep voice, as he gazed out at the parking lot. "You will, if you look, but not always quite the thing you were after."

"That's not how it goes," said Keyton, who ought to know, it being one of zir favorite quotes from *The Hobbit*.

"Customized for you," Nicholas said, grinning.

For a while after that, there was silence. But with their hands clasped, it was actually very loud. Like music.

TWENTY-NINE

It was Sunday. Rufus sat on the picnic bench, his back to the table. He was feeling good, because after two months of him campaigning, his mother had finally given in and agreed to try adding wasabi to her potato salad.

Now she stood by the food table, and Rufus could hear Mr. Hutherson saying how it was maybe the best potato salad he'd ever had, and what had she changed?

Rufus's mother was acting modest, the way she did, while at the same time managing to not answer his question at all.

Smooth.

Rufus took another bite of his mother's work. It was excellent, if he did say so himself. He pulled his mobile from his jacket. Again.

Nothing. He tucked it back into the pocket.

"Hey, dimwit," said William, who sat at his side. William set a small square tin on the bench between them.

"Oh, cool," said Rufus, picking up the red and white metal tin of mastic chewing gum.

William laughed. "Of course you know what it is."

"Sure do," Rufus said.

"You're welcome," William said. "Also, thanks."

"For what?"

"For Diane. After you told her that you were dating someone, she was a whole lot more willing to talk with me. Now I've got a date for Lupine Middle School prom."

"Nice," said Rufus, happy for his friend.

"Oh yeah," William said with feeling. "So you're dating someone?"

"No. And I didn't say that. I just told her there's a girl I like. She decided it meant something else."

"Good trick. So is there a girl or not?"

Rufus sighed, turning the red and white tin between his fingers, the pieces of gum making clicking sounds against the metal. He looked at the gathered adults and kids, the pastor in the corner by the dessert table, and wondered if he could get away with chewing gum here.

Probably not. He tucked the tin into his other jacket pocket.

"Not yet."

"You're kidding me. Ask her out, man."

"I did. I'm waiting for an answer."

"Waiting? How long you been waiting?"

"Two weeks."

William shook his head. "Ask again, cadet."

"She heard me the first time. She'll answer when she's ready."

"If she doesn't forget."

"She won't," Rufus said. "She's not like that."

"Man. She must be really pretty."

"Yep," Rufus said, and pulled out his phone again. "Blast it, she just texted me, and I missed it. She says..."

His face went blank.

"What? What did she say?" William asked.

Rufus felt an odd buzz, like he was the phone, and it was buzzing.

Suddenly, he couldn't speak. He tried, but all that came out was a croaking sound.

"Hah?" William asked.

The world had just shifted a bit, Rufus guessed. The future had changed.

"Yes," Rufus said. "She said yes."

William grinned and slapped Rufus's shoulder. "Epic."

CHAPTER

THIRTY

It rained for two days after the ring went home. To Sanne, it felt like a warm shower for her spirit, helping her to recover from the prior excitement.

The kids returned to school. By the end of the week, they resumed lessons with Sanne. Routine seemed to re-establish itself.

With some changes.

Of all the surprises to come out of the successful quest to get the ring home, the new and tingling tension between Angie and Rufus—spark to flame of deeper affection—was one of the most unexpected. Sanne would never have guessed.

But then, you never could about such things.

That alone would have been plenty for the group to hold. Then a few days later, the Fates saw fit to expand the group, when Nicholas joined them.

Now there were two sets of tingling tensions in the room, and Sanne needed to bring in new sorts of calming spells. It wouldn't be long, she suspected, for those spells to find their way into the group's unofficial curriculum.

They were all getting along well, so far, which was not something you could magic into existence. It took work, luck, and —sooner or later, no doubt—more listening circles.

For the moment, though, all was well, and Sanne was content to have her finger free of a trapped spirit in a wayward ring.

This morning, Sanne had slept deliciously late. A mug of coffee nestled warmly in one hand while the rich scent of brew filled the room. Sanne sat at the table, content to watch the pattering rain cascade down skylights and windows.

From her phone, she heard the trilling call of a spotted towhee. Sanne sensed into the caller's energy, which—if she were to think in terms of food, as Rufus might—had the distinct flavor of her sister Marla.

She answered.

"Got my calendar in front of me," Marla said without preamble. "I can visit you next month. Work for you?"

"You're coming out?" Sanne asked delightedly.

"That's the plan, big sis'. Been too long. Okay for me to bring a friend?"

Sanne's eyebrows shot up. She smiled wide. "You've got a new beau? And you want me to meet him?"

There was silence.

"Marla?" asked Sanne, her smile slowly fading.

Marla cleared her throat. "Some interesting times around here lately. I put my best PI on him. Did a deep dive into his finances. Also—"

"Wait, wait," interrupted Sanne. "Who are you—are you talking about—"

"Allen, yeah. He's our brother, all right."

"No way."

"Way."

"No, I mean, no way *you*," Sanne said. "You told me not to talk to him. At all. 'Heart and sense of a baby fawn.' Remember that part?"

"If you had any idea what I put him through—" Marla began.

"I can imagine," Sanne said dryly. "But when I wanted to talk to him—"

"You're gullible. And so open-hearted that ventricles slide out. I'm not. Admit it."

"I am," Sanne said after a moment's self-assessment. "And I intend to stay that way."

"Then I intend to stay suspicious and adversarial."

"Good division of labor," Sanne said. "So, Allen?"

"Genetic testing says full sibling."

Sanne inhaled sharply, held it a moment, let it out in a long stream, feeling the effect of Marla's words.

"I know," Marla said, reading Sanne's thoughts. "I was worried there might have been an affair, too. But no—he's both our parents' child, adopted out. Six years older than us. Mom and dad would have been in high school."

"High school," Sanne echoed. "But wait, you said you didn't care if he was the real thing. That he was just after our money."

"I was wrong," Marla said matter-of-factly. "He's got money."

"But why contact us now?"

"Vermont state law changed last year to allow adoptees new info if their parents were deceased. From that, he got a last name. Then he found an article about you and your wildcrafting classes."

"Ah-ha! I knew the wildcrafting would pay off someday. See? Now we have a brother. You can thank me later." Sanne was trying to make light.

"We have a brother," Marla said with gravity.

"What's he like?"

Sanne could hear the smile in Marla's voice. "Kind of a hybrid between you and me. IP lawyer and practicing Buddhist."

"You already like him."

"I guess I do. So far. Clearly don't I know him well enough yet," she quipped. "Oh, and—like our parents, he's happily married. Also, he has kids."

"Kids?" Neither she nor Marla had any. "Oh my gosh," said Sanne.

"Yeah. A boy and a girl. Sanne, we're aunts."

Sanne inhaled again. It was a lot. "How old are they?"

Another pause. A long pause.

"Marla?"

"Ten and eleven," Marla answered.

Sanne felt the blood drain from her head. It was the very same age Marla and Sanne had been when their parents had been killed.

Did it mean anything? Of course not. And yet...

"Sanne, could you maybe..." Marla said, her voice quiet and tone hesitant, completely unlike her. "Could you maybe do a protection spell or something for them?"

"Sis. You don't believe this stuff."

"I'm ready to suspend my disbelief, if there's even a chance it works."

For a moment, Sanne considered telling Marla about the demon eggs that Marla had inadvertently sent Sanne last Spring, and how Sanne, her three teens, and Della, had done some substantial spellcraft to take care of that little problem. Three not-so-little problems.

Or how Sanne and her three teenagers had just freed a trapped spirit and returned a cherished ring to a father and son who were at last beginning to heal.

Sanne imagined asking the three teens—four, now—if they'd be willing to help her create protection spells for this new sibling of hers, and his two children. She knew what they'd say: when do we start?

"Yes," Sanne told her sister. "I will."

In that moment, Sanne sensed a crack in her sister's willingness to know more about Sanne's world, something they usually didn't discuss.

And your sister, too. Make sure she knows.

"Marla, there's something I need to tell you."

"What's that?"

How to explain?

"It's been an interesting time around here, too. You see, I

found this ring. A blue star sapphire. One thing led to another, and...well. I have a message for you."

A Message From The Author

Thanks for joining me on this adventure!

When you read a story, you are an essential part of what makes it come alive. If you liked this story, say so. Tell others. Tell me, even! We authors do our best work when we know it's touched someone.

Ratings also make a huge difference. A note to a friend, a good review, a rating—these are precious gifts that also help us create more stories. Thank you!

ALSO BY SONIA ORIN LYRIS

"Treasure Twice Over," *Witches, Cutter's Final Cut: Issue Four.* Join Sanne for some magical adventure in the Marigold library!

The Seer Saga, (The Seer, Unmoored, Maelstrom, Landfall), an immersive high fantasy series

Better Selves, a collection of science fiction and urban fantasy stories, with afterword by Barry N. Malzberg

"When Strangers Meet," Dispatches from Anarres, tales in tribute to Ursula K. Le Guin

ABOUT THE AUTHOR

Sonia Orin Lyris writes stories about strong women and the men who can see them. Her writing has been called "immersive" and "unsparing."

She is the author of *The Seer Saga*, an epic high-fantasy series that asks questions about power and love. She is co-creator of *Rochi*, a divination and gambling game with vivid artwork.

Her hobbies include partner dance, martial arts, fine chocolate, and feline poetry.

WANT MORE?

Follow me on Patreon for juicy notes, or subscribe for confessional posts. https://www.patreon.com/lyris

For concise updates, check my Facebook feed. https://www.facebook.com/authorlyris

My newsletter is infrequent but excellently informative. Sign up here. https://lyris.org/subscribe/

All my newest works, all in one place: https://lyris.org/newly-published/

More at my website. https://lyris.org/